the winter of candy canes

Other Books in the Sweet Season Series

The Summer of Cotton Candy

The Fall of Candy Corn

A Sweet Seasons Novel

the winter of candy canes

debbie viguié

ZONDERVAN®

ZONDERVAN.com/
AUTHORTRACKER
follow your favorite authors

To all those who work to make others' vacations so enjoyable. Thank you to my family, friends, and the wonderful group at Zonderkidz. Without you none of this would be possible.

The Winter of Candy Canes
Copyright © 2008 by Debbie Viguie

Requests for information should be addressed to:
Zondervan, *Grand Rapids, Michigan 49530*

Library of Congress Cataloging-in-Publication Data: Applied for

ISBN 978-0-310-71752-2

Published in association with the literary agency of Alive Communications, Inc., 7680 Goddard Street, Suite 200, Colorado Springs, Colorado 80920. www.alivecommunications.com

Interior design by Christine Orejuela-Winkelman

Printed in the United States of America

08 09 10 11 12 13 14 • 23 22 21 20 19 18 17 16 15 14 13 12 11 10 9 8 7 6 5 4 3 2 1

the winter of candy canes

1

Candace Thompson was once again eye-to-eye with Lloyd Peterson, hiring manager for The Zone theme park. This time, though, she felt far more confident. She had already spent her summer working as a cotton candy vendor, and she had worked one of the mazes for the annual Halloween event. She had even saved the park from saboteurs.

Now she was back, and this time she was interviewing for a job working the Christmas events at the park. Surely after everything she had done for the Scare event, she had nothing to worry about. She tucked a strand of red hair back behind her ear as she gazed intently at the man across from her.

"So you want to work Holly Daze?" he asked.

She nodded. Christmas at The Zone was a big deal, and the park began its official celebrations the day after Thanksgiving.

"You keep hiring on for short bursts of time and then leaving. Do you have some sort of problem committing to things?" he asked, staring hard at her.

She was stunned, but answered, "I don't have any problem with commitment. I signed on to do specific things, and the jobs ended. That's not my fault. I didn't quit."

"So, you plan on making a habit of this?" he demanded. "Are you going to show up here again in a couple of months expecting me to give you some kind of job for spring break?"

"No, I—"

"I know your type," he said, standing up abruptly. "You're just a party girl. No commitments ... no cares ... just grab some quick cash and get out. You think you can handle Holly Daze? Well, you can't! You're weak and a quitter. You're going to bail on me as soon as your school vacation starts, and then what? Well, let me tell you, missy. You aren't wanted here. So just pack your bags and get out!"

By the end of his tirade, he was shouting, eyes bulging behind his glasses and tie swinging wildly as he shook his finger under her nose. Candace recoiled, sure that he had finally flipped out. *I'm going to end up as a headline*: *Girl Murdered by Stressed-Out Recruiter,* she thought wildly. *Well, I'm not going down without a fight!* She jumped to her feet and put some distance between her and the wildly wagging finger.

"You need to calm down!" she said, projecting her voice like her drama teacher had taught her. Her voice seemed to boom in the tiny office. "Pull yourself together. You're a representative of this theme park, and there is no call to insult me. Furthermore, I'm not a quitter. I'll work for the entire Christmas season. Then the next time I come in here, I'll expect you to treat me with some respect. Do you even realize what I've done for this park so far? Seriously. Take a chill pill."

She stopped speaking when she realized that he had gone completely quiet. She held her breath, wondering when the next explosion was going to come. Instead, he sat down abruptly and waved her back to her chair.

"Very good. You passed the test," he said, picking up a pen.

"What test?" she asked, edging her way back into the chair.

"The ultimate test. You're going to be one of Santa's elves."

"Doesn't Santa, you know, have his own elves?" she asked, still not sure that he was completely in charge of his senses.

"Of course Santa has his own elves. However, when he's here at The Zone we supply him with courtesy elves so that they can continue making toys at the North Pole," Mr. Peterson told her.

"So, I'm going to be a courtesy elf?" she asked.

He nodded and handed her a single sheet of paper. "Sign this."

She took it. "What? Just one thing to sign?" She had expected another huge stack of forms that would leave her hand cramped for hours afterward.

He nodded curtly. "You're now in our system as a regular seasonal employee. All of your other paperwork transfers."

"Regular seasonal" sounded like some kind of contradiction to her, but she was still not entirely convinced his outburst had been a test. She scanned it, signed her name, and then handed it back to him.

"Good. Report to wardrobe on Saturday for your costume fitting," he said.

"Okay, thank you," she said, standing up and backing toward the door.

"Welcome back, Candy," he said, smiling faintly.

"Thanks," she said, before bolting out the door.

As soon as she was outside the building, she whipped out her cell phone and called her friend Josh, a fellow employee of The Zone.

"Well?" he asked when he picked up.

"I think Mr. Peterson has seriously lost it," she said. "He totally flipped out on me."

Josh laughed. "Let me guess. You're going to be an elf."

"So he was serious? That was some whacked-out test?"

"Yeah. Elves are considered a class-one stress position, and it can get pretty intense."

"How hard can it be to be an elf?" she asked.

She was rewarded by a burst of laughter on the other end.

"Josh, what is it you're not telling me?"

He just kept laughing.

"Okay, seriously. You were the one who convinced me to work Holly Daze. I think it's only fair you tell me whatever it is I need to know."

"Sorry!" he gasped. She wasn't sure if he was apologizing or refusing to tell her.

A girl bounced around the corner and slammed into Candace.

"Josh, I'll call you later," she said, hanging up.

"Sorry," Becca apologized.

Becca was one of Candace's other friends from the park, one who had some sort of bizarre allergy to sugar that made her uncontrollably hyper. Candace looked suspiciously at Becca. Her cheeks were flushed, her eyes were glistening, and she was hopping from one foot to the other.

"You didn't have sugar, did you?" Candace asked, fear ripping through her.

"No! Promise," Becca said.

"Then what gives?"

"Roger made me laugh really hard," Becca explained.

Roger had a crush on Becca and had wanted to ask her out since Halloween. It hadn't happened yet.

"Oh," was all Candace could think to say.

"So, are you working Holly Daze?" Becca asked.

"Yeah. I'm going to be an elf."

Suddenly, Becca went completely still, and the smile left her face. "I'm sorry," she said.

"Why?" Candace asked.

Becca just shook her head. "I've gotta get back to the Muffin Mansion. I'll catch you later."

She hurried off, and Candace watched her go. *Okay, now I know there's something people aren't telling me.*

She debated about following Becca and forcing her to spill, but instead she headed for the parking lot where her best friend Tamara was waiting. She walked through the Exploration Zone, one of the several themed areas in the park.

The Zone theme park was created and owned by John Hanson, a former professional quarterback who believed in healthy competition at work and play. His theme park had several areas, or zones, where people could compete with each other and themselves at just about anything. Almost everyone who worked at The Zone was called a referee. The exceptions were the costumed characters called mascots. Most of them, including Candace's boyfriend, Kurt, were to be found in the History Zone. People visiting the park were called players, and the areas of the park they could reach were called on field. Only refs could go off field.

Candace cut through an off field area to get to the referee parking lot. She waved at a few other people she recognized from her time spent working there. Finally, she slid into her friend's waiting car.

"So are you going to be the Christmas queen?" Tamara asked.

"What am I, Lucy VanPelt? There's no Christmas queen in Charlie Brown's Christmas play, and there's no Christmas queen in The Zone," Candace said.

Tamara fake pouted. "Are you sure? I think I'd make a beautiful Christmas queen."

Candace laughed. Tamara was gorgeous, rich, and fun. Her whole family practically redefined the word *wealthy*, and, with her dark hair and olive skin, Tamara was usually the prettiest girl in any room. She didn't let it go to her head, though. Anybody who knew Tamara would vote for her as Christmas queen.

"Although I think you would, they're only hiring elves."

"You're going to be an elf?" Tamara smirked.

"Hey, it beats being a food cart vendor," Candace said.

"But you're so good at it. Cotton candy, candy corn . . . you can sell it all."

"Thanks, I think. So, what are we doing tonight? Kurt's going to swing by at six to pick us up." Just mentioning her boyfriend's name was enough to make Candace smile. She closed her eyes for just a minute and pictured him as she had first seen him—wearing a Lone Ranger costume. With his charm and piercing blue eyes, she had fallen for him right away.

"You told him my house, right?" Tamara said, interrupting her thoughts.

"Yeah. So, who's this guy you're taking?"

Tamara sighed. "Mark."

"Uh-huh. And?"

"Remember my cousin Tina?"

"Yeah."

"Well, she broke up with him over the summer, and he's been all shattered since then. He won't date other girls; he just mopes over her."

"Attractive," Candace said sarcastically.

"Tell me about it. Well, Tina asked me if I could help him get his confidence back and get over her or something."

"A pity date? Are you kidding me? You want Kurt and I to double date with you on a pity date?"

"You don't think I'm about to go by myself, do you? No way. That's the best-friend creed. When you're happy, I'm happy. When I'm miserable, you have to be too."

"Great," Candace said, rolling her eyes. "So, where are we going?"

"That's the problem. I was thinking dinner, but then we'd have to talk, and frankly, I don't want to hear him go on about Tina. Then I thought we could see a movie."

"You wouldn't have to talk to him," Candace confirmed.

"Yeah, but what if—"

"He tries to grab a hand or put his arm around you."

"Exactly, and I don't think me giving him a black eye was what Tina had in mind."

"I guess that also rules out any kind of concert possibilities?" Candace asked wistfully.

"Yup. Sorry."

"So, what did you come up with?"

"I was thinking . . . theme park?"

"No way. Kurt doesn't like to spend his downtime there."

"I thought he took you to that romantic dinner there over the summer."

"It was the nicest restaurant he knew, and he got an employee discount."

"Charming," Tamara said.

"Plus, ever since we got trapped in there overnight, he's been even more adamant about avoiding it when he's off work."

"I can't believe you two get to be the stuff of urban legend, and you don't even appreciate it."

Candace sighed. It was true that she and Kurt had spent one of the most miserable nights of their relationship trapped inside the theme park. Urban legend, though, had since transformed the story so that they were supposedly chased through the park by a psycho killer. It was still embarrassing to have people point at her and say that she was the one. Around Halloween she had given up trying to correct people. They were going to believe what they wanted.

"Earth to Candace. Helloooo?"

"Sorry. So, what does that leave us with? Shopping?"

"No need to torture both our dates," Tamara said.

"Then what?"

"I don't—miniature golf!" Tamara suddenly shrieked, so loudly that Candace jumped and slammed her head into the roof of the car.

"Tam! Don't scare me like that."

"Sorry. Miniature golf. What do you think? Built-in talking points, lots of movement, and zero grabby potential."

"I like it. I'll have to borrow one of your jackets though."

"At least you'll have an actual excuse this time," Tamara teased.

A few minutes later they were at Tamara's house and upstairs raiding her wardrobe. As Tamara considered and discarded a fifth outfit, Candace threw up her hands.

"Maybe if you'd tell me what you're looking for, I could help."

"I'm looking for something, you know, nunlike."

Candace stared at her friend for a moment before she burst out laughing. She fell to the floor, clutching her stomach as tears streamed down her face. Tamara crossed her arms and tapped her foot, and Candace just laughed harder.

"I don't know why you think that's so funny. You know I don't go past kissing."

"Tam, nuns can't even do that. And if you're looking for something that will completely hide your body, then you're going to have to go to the mall instead of the closet. You don't own anything that doesn't say 'look at me.' I'm sorry, but it's true."

"Really? Maybe we should go to your house. Think I could find what I'm looking for in your closet?"

"Not since I started dating and mom made me throw out all my old camp T-shirts," Candace said with a grin.

"Then hello, you've got no call to laugh."

Candace stood up, stomach still aching from laughing so hard. "Tam, I'm not criticizing. I'm just telling you, you're not going to find what you're looking for."

Tam reached into the closet. "Oh, yeah, what about this?" she asked, producing jeans and a black turtleneck.

"If you're going for the secret agent look, it's a good choice."

Tamara threw the jeans at her, and Candace ducked.

"I could wear some black pants with this. Would that be too funereal?

"For a pity date? Go for it."

Candace opted to borrow Tamara's discarded jeans instead of wearing the skirt she had brought with her. They turned out to be slightly tighter on her than they were on Tam, and she had to admit when she paired them with her red scoop-neck top that she looked really good.

When Kurt arrived a few minutes later, he whistled when he saw her.

"Keep the jeans," Tamara whispered to her. "Obviously, they work for you."

Kurt then looked at Tamara and frowned slightly. "Did you just come from a funeral?"

"No, but thank you for thinking so," Tamara said with a smirk.

"I don't—"

Candace put her finger over his lips. "Don't ask," she advised him.

He smiled and kissed her finger, which made her giggle.

The doorbell rang again, and Candace turned, eager to see the infamous Mark.

Tamara opened the door, and Candace sucked in her breath. Mark was gorgeous. He had auburn hair, piercing green eyes, and model-perfect features. He was almost as tall as Kurt, and he was stunning in khaki Dockers and a green Polo shirt.

"Hi," he said, smiling.

Tamara glanced at her and rolled her eyes.

"Hi, Mark."

Kurt drove, and Candace was quick to slide into the front seat with him, leaving Tamara and Mark to the back. She shook her head. Mark was not her idea of a pity date in any sense of the word. Maybe Tamara would come around if she actually talked to him.

They made it to the miniature golf course and were soon on the green. Candace got a hole in one on the first time up to putt, and Kurt gave her a huge reward kiss.

When they moved on to the next hole, Tamara whispered in her ear, "Thanks a lot. This is supposed to be a no grabby zone. Now Mark will be getting ideas."

"Tam, you really need to relax a little."

They made it through the course in record time, and Kurt gave Candace another kiss for winning by one stroke. After turning in

15

their clubs, the guys headed inside to order pizza while Candace and Tamara went to the restroom.

"This date is the worst," Tamara groaned once they were alone.

"What's wrong with you? He's gorgeous."

"Really? I guess I just can't see past the Tina mope."

"What mope? He hasn't even mentioned her, and he's done nothing but smile all night. You should totally take him to Winter Formal."

"No way. This is a one-date-only kind of thing. I'm not taking him to Winter Formal."

"Fine. Suit yourself. I'm just telling you that if it weren't for Kurt, I'd be taking him to Winter Formal."

Tamara laughed.

"As if. There's no way you'd ask a guy out."

"I don't know. You might be surprised."

"It's a moot point anyway. I'll find someone to take."

"You could always take Josh," Candace suggested.

"You're not setting me up with Josh, so just forget it."

"Fine."

"Find out for me, though, if Santa needs a Mrs. Claus," Tamara said.

"You're going to find some way to be the Christmas queen, aren't you?" Candace asked.

"Even if I have to marry old Saint Nick."

They both laughed.

2

On Saturday morning Candace reported to the wardrobe area to get fitted for her elf costume. She was surprised to see Kurt there.

"What are you doing here?"

He smiled. "I'm here to speak to the elves. It's the only time you're all going to be gathered together."

"Why do you need to speak to us elves?" she asked, momentarily distracted as she saw Lisa walk in, flipping her blonde hair. *Seriously, she's not going to be an elf*, Candace thought in despair. Lisa had been a thorn in Candace's side for months. She was Kurt's ex-girlfriend and not at all happy about the "ex" part. Lisa glared in Candace's direction, and Candace grimaced, fighting the urge to say something rude.

"Candace, you listening?" Kurt asked.

"Sorry, what were you saying?"

"I'm here to talk to all the elves. You see, as an elf, you're part normal referee, part crowd control, and part costumed mascot."

"So, you're here to give us a mascot pep talk?"

"Something like that."

"How hard can being an elf actually be?" she asked, more to herself than him.

"You're kidding, right?"

"What do you mean?"

"Elves get hazard pay."

"Seriously?" she asked. The recruiter had failed to mention that. Half of her was wondering how much more money she would see in her paycheck, and the other half was now really worried. What on earth would merit hazard pay at a theme park during Christmas?

"Seriously," Kurt confirmed. "I did it last year. Never again."

Before she could ask him anything else, the head of the costuming department, Janet, clapped her hands and called everyone to attention. "All right, go ahead and take a seat if you can find one. Hit the floor if you can't," she instructed.

"I'm on," Kurt said, walking toward Janet.

Candace sat down on the floor, envying Lisa the folding chair she had acquired. Candace glanced around. There were about thirty people present besides Kurt and Janet. She thought she recognized one or two of them from Scare, but Lisa was the only one she knew by name.

"This is Kurt, one of our outstanding mascots who works in the History Zone. He's here to give you some instruction, some ground rules, and some survival tips," Janet said without even a hint of a smile.

Candace initiated a brief round of applause. Kurt winked at her, and she blushed.

"Out in the park, I play Robin Hood, Zorro, the Lone Ranger, and occasionally others. Last Christmas I was sitting where you're sitting, ready for elf orientation. I figured because I was a mascot being an elf would be a piece of cake. I was wrong."

His tone had become increasingly grim, and Candace shivered. *What in the world have I gotten myself into?* she wondered.

"You are the last line of defense. You are all that stands between thousands of excited, frightened, hopeful kids and Santa Claus. And they will go around you, over you, and through you to get to him. Last year an elf tripped and fell, and five hundred kids trampled him. He got out of the hospital last month."

Around her, people stirred and muttered to each other in frightened tones. Candace had to admit that her own heart was starting to race in fear. This had to be why Josh had said it was a level-one stress job.

"So, here are a few tips. Rule number one. Remember, you're the adults. What you say goes. Don't let them intimidate you. Also, don't let their parents intimidate you. Just follow your procedures. Make sure you call for security if they try to mob Santa."

Candace noticed that several people near her were looking pale and nervous. She didn't blame them. She didn't like the sound of things either. She also wondered vaguely when she had become an "adult." She was only seventeen, and that didn't qualify her as an adult anywhere else in the world.

"Rule number two. Remember to keep smiling. It's what we do here at The Zone. It also helps diffuse tense situations and gets people to relax. Grumpy elves lead to cranky children and impatient parents. No one wants that."

Kurt flashed a giant smile as an example, and Candace noted that most people instantly smiled back.

"Rule number three. You're also representing Santa. Don't make him look bad. Christmas time at The Zone should make happy memories for the children who come here."

Heads were bobbing all around the room. Candace wasn't the only one who had come to see Santa at the theme park when she was younger.

"Rule number four. No one gets candy canes until after they've seen Santa. This means they sugar up on their way out, and Santa doesn't get candy stuck in his beard and blame us for providing poor elf service."

Candace thought of Becca and wondered if there'd ever been any incidents with her friend and the candy canes.

Becca's sugar-hyped exploits in the park seemed to be legion in number and epic in scale.

"And the most important rule in The Zone is …?" Kurt asked, cupping his hand behind his ear.

"Let players play," Candace chorused with everyone else.

"Excellent. Good luck to you all. I'll debrief the survivors on the other side."

"Thank you, Kurt," Janet said as he moved to sit on the floor next to Candace.

"You were great," Candace gushed, "although now I'm terrified."

"Then I did my job," he said.

Elves began to scatter to different costumers as the fittings began. Candace stood slowly, savoring the moments alone with Kurt. "That story about the referee who got trampled—is that true?" she asked, suspiciously.

He grinned. "I have no idea. They told me that story last year, and it scared the daylights out of me."

"Just another urban legend you're promoting?" she teased.

"You know me."

She smiled, but there was something else on her mind. "I've got a question for you."

"What?"

"I was just wondering, if you don't have any plans, would you like to come have Thanksgiving with my family?"

He hesitated.

"It's not like there'll be a spotlight on you or anything," Candace hastened to say. "There are always loads of people. I think Mom's expecting thirty this year."

He nodded slowly. "Yeah, okay. Thanks."

"So, you'll be there?" she asked.

"I'm working until one that day."

"Dinner's at two."

"Then I'll be there," he said.

"Great!" she said, a little more enthusiastically than she had meant to. While she was excited at the idea of spending Thanksgiving with him, her parents had really pushed for it. Still, with so many people around, it wasn't like they could put Kurt in the hot seat.

"Candy!" Janet called.

Ready to be transformed into an elf, she ran over to Janet.

Fortunately, when she tried it on, her costume seemed to fit just right. Candace turned in front of the mirror. She was wearing a glitter-covered green dress that ended a couple inches above her knees along with red tights and green pointed-toe shoes. It was by far the best uniform she'd had while working at The Zone.

"Will I be wearing a hat?" she asked Janet.

The woman shook her head. "Boys wear hats; girls wear these," she said, handing Candace a wreath of glittery green holly.

"Cool."

"It should look really nice with your red hair. You're all set for Christmas," Janet said.

"Thanks."

"And in case the temperature drops too low, we have these green velvet coats lined with white fake fur," Janet said, showing her one.

"At least I'll look festive," she said, turning once more in front of the mirror.

"There you are!"

Candace turned and saw Martha, one of the supervisors, bustling toward her.

"Hey, Martha!" Candace said, giving the older woman a quick hug.

"Don't you look like Miss Christmas yourself," Martha said with a smile, her gravelly voice seeming even a little deeper than it had a few weeks before. "I see you opted to go the elf route."

"Josh talked me into it," Candace admitted.

"That one's got a bit of mischief in him," Martha said with a smile. "I notice he didn't sign up to be an elf."

Candace shrugged. "I'll just have to find some way to pay him back."

"That's the spirit."

"So, what's up?"

"I'm trying to catch all the elves to give them their schedules," Martha said, handing Candace a piece of paper. "This is when you'll be working. All the excitement will start bright and early at seven a.m. the day after Thanksgiving."

"I didn't think the park opened that early," Candace said. She had never had to report to the park before eight a.m.

"Park opens at eight, but elves need to be in place and briefed before then."

"Ah."

"I know. Who needs to sleep in?" Martha said, shaking her head.

"It's cool. Last year I was at the mall with my mom at four a.m.," Candace said with a shudder.

"You'll probably wish you were there again," Martha said grimly.

Candace smiled at her. Martha smiled back. "But you'll do fine," Martha hastened to assure her.

Wow, it really does work, Candace thought. *I might just have to spend the entire season smiling.*

❄

Monday at lunch, Candace and Tamara were sitting together at a table with a bunch of other girls. Everyone had been driven inside by a steady drizzle of rain all morning. Inside the cafeteria, the only topic of conversation was Winter Formal.

"Who are you going with, Candace?" one of the girls asked.

"I'm taking my boyfriend, Kurt," Candace said, pride in her voice. "He's in college."

"And he's gorgeous," Tamara added, as though on cue.

"Ohhh," several of the girls chorused. It was nice for a change to be one of the girls with a guaranteed date. It definitely put her in the minority at the table.

"So, Tam, who are you taking?" Candace asked.

"Still haven't decided," Tamara admitted.

"Didn't Bryce ask you?" one of the girls said.

"Didn't half the football team?" another quipped.

"Yeah, but it's the other half I'm interested in," Tamara joked.

"Seriously, Tamara, you could have any guy here you wanted," another said enviously.

"I guess that's the problem. I don't want any of them here," Tamara said.

"I'm telling you, you should ask Josh," Candace said.

"Will you lay off the Josh thing?" Tamara said with a roll of her eyes. "I've told you. He's a great guy, but it's just not … right."

"I totally get that," Stefanie, the queen of the airheads gushed. "When it's not right it's … like … it's … I don't know, wrong."

Candace bit her lip to keep from laughing.

"What she said," Tamara sighed.

"I guess that's okay. There's always Mark."

For a moment she thought Tamara was going to throw her soda in Candace's face.

"That is soooo not funny."

"Mark who?" Stefanie asked.

"Mark so-not-going-with-me, that's who."

"Oh."

"Change the subject," Tamara warned.

Candace smiled. "Kurt's coming to my house for Thanksgiving."

That got the attention of the whole table.

"No way! Bringing the boyfriend to a family function?"

"You are so brave."

"My boyfriend swears he'll never be in the same room as my parents."

"What's the big deal?" Candace asked. "It's just dinner, and there'll be lots of people there."

"Are you serious?" Tamara asked. "Having the boyfriend officially meet your parents, spend some time with them, share the *family* meal. That's totally major."

"It's like you're saying he's the one," Stefanie said solemnly.

"Is he the one?" several of the others asked in unison.

"The one what?"

"That you're going to marry," Tanya said with a shake of her head.

"No! What? I don't know. I haven't even graduated from high school yet. Marriage is way far down the road."

"But you think about it, right?" Kayla asked, a dreamy look on her face.

Kayla was the other one in the group with a steady boyfriend. Clearly she did think about marrying her guy. Candace thought about it sometimes too. Well, she more worried about it than thought about it. "I don't even know if Kurt's right for me."

Suddenly, there were eight other girls eager to help her figure that out. Tanya even pulled a compatibility quiz out of her backpack.

"Good going," Tamara said with a smile.

"At least they're not talking about you any more," Candace growled.

"Yup. Life is good."

Fortunately, lunch was soon over, and the next classes flew by until the last period of the day arrived. Candace met back up with Tamara in the auditorium for drama.

It turned out Mr. Bailey had a surprise for them. "We're going to be holding auditions for the spring play before Christmas vacation this year. I realize it's a break with tradition, but we're going to need to hit the ground running with this particular production. Auditions are going to be held in three weeks."

"What play?" Jill, one of the sophomores, asked.

"Ah, that's the exciting part. We'll be doing a musical this year—"

Before he could say which one, Jill jumped to her feet and shrieked, "Yes!" Several of the other girls started muttering excitedly.

Mr. Bailey cleared his throat and projected his voice above the din. "And it's not *High School Musical*."

Jill groaned in despair and slumped back into her chair. Candace bit her lip to keep from laughing.

"We'll be doing *Man of La Mancha*—the story of a brave man, Don Quixote, who takes on the role of becoming a knight and ignores the criticism and interference of others in his pursuit of the impossible dream."

Candace felt an instant sense of relief. If she remembered correctly, there were really only three female roles in the play. Dressing up in costume and being on display at The Zone was one thing; being on stage and forgetting her lines was quite another.

"I bet you play the lead," Candace whispered to Tamara.

"Who says I even want it?" Tamara shot back.

"Drama was your idea, remember?"

"Only vaguely. It seemed like a good idea at the time."

"Famous last words."

"Those of you who are not cast in one of the roles will still get to be in *Man of La Mancha* as part of the chorus," Mr. Bailey said.

Candace stifled a groan. It looked like one way or another she was going to end up on stage.

"Not only will everyone get a chance to be on stage, but everyone will also get a chance to construct sets, work on costumes, and learn all about stage makeup."

At the last part, all the guys in the room made faces, and all the girls giggled.

"Now that will be worth seeing!" Tamara laughed.

3

As soon as class was over, they made their way to Tamara's car.

"Girl, we are going shopping," Tamara announced once she pulled out of the parking lot.

"What kind of shopping?"

"Christmas."

"Isn't it a little early?" Candace asked. "The sales don't start until Friday."

"Yeah, and you're working Friday, right?"

"Yeah, but—"

"But nothing. I figure I can write you off for most of the season thanks to The Zone. Not that I'm complaining," she hastened to add. "I just want to get some of our annual Christmas shopping madness taken care of while we can."

"But I'm not even dressed for it," Candace protested.

"Tough. I'll buy you something to wear while we do the rest of our shopping," Tamara said, jaw clenched.

Candace just laughed. "Okay, then, lead on." She grabbed her cell phone and left a brief message for her parents, letting them know that she was going to be out late with Tamara.

A few minutes later they were inside the mall, and Candace shook her head as she took in all the decorations. "Looks like the mall's already in full holiday swing," she said.

"Yeah, and look," Tamara said pointing to some huge signs in one window. "You were afraid they were going to wait until Friday to start all the sales."

Candace grinned. "Christmas comes earlier every year."

"Or at least the marketing does," Tamara finished. "So, who's on your list?"

"Everyone. I've done zero shopping so far."

"Me too."

They walked slowly past a variety of shops and stared at the items in the windows.

"What are you getting Kurt?" Tamara asked.

"I don't know. It's driving me crazy, actually. I don't know whether to give him something silly and romantic or something practical that he could really use or something he really wants."

"What does he really want?"

"I don't know!"

"Have you tried asking him?"

"I'm trying to be sneaky. I want him to be surprised, you know?"

"Get him tickets to something. What's his favorite team?"

"I don't know," Candace admitted.

"Okay, favorite sport?"

"Again, don't know."

"Hmmm. Is there something he's always wanted to do, like sky dive or go to Paris?"

Candace laughed. "I don't know, and even if he did, that would be way, way out of my budget. I'm thinking under fifty bucks."

"You usually spend more on my presents," Tamara said.

"That's because I'm using *your* credit card when I buy your presents."

"Oh yeah," Tamara said with a smile.

"Go with silly and romantic," Tamara advised after a minute. "It'll be easier, and it'll be cute."

"What do you have in mind?"

They stopped at a kiosk in the middle of the mall. "Get him a mouse pad with your picture on it," Tamara suggested, waving toward a display.

"Maybe ... I don't know. It just doesn't seem quite right. Besides, I'm not sure how much he uses a computer."

"Then get a mug. I'm sure he uses those," Tamara said.

"That just doesn't seem romantic or useful or interesting," Candace sighed.

"Hey, don't we know that sad sack of misery over there?" Tamara asked, pointing toward a guy seated on one of the planters with his head in his hands and his shoulders slumped in defeat.

"It looks like Roger," Candace said.

"More like the empty husk of what was Roger. Why does he look like that?"

"I don't know. Let's find out," Candace said, already headed toward him.

"Hey, Roger, you okay?" Candace asked when they were standing next to him.

He looked up, startled. "Oh, hi, Candy. No, I'm not okay."

"What's wrong?" Tamara asked.

"I can't even work up the nerve to ask Becca out. How am I supposed to figure out what to get her for Christmas?"

"You know, I thought you were going to ask her out the day after Halloween. It's been weeks. What happened?"

"I know. It's just that every time I'm about to, I look into her beautiful, crazy, scary blue eyes, and I can't do it. I chicken out."

"Are you afraid she'll say no?" Candace asked.

"Or are you afraid she'll break every bone in your body next time she's on a sugar rush?" Tamara suggested.

"No, I know at some point I'll get hurt; that's a risk I'm willing to take to be with her. I'm just afraid she doesn't like me in the same way."

"Only one way to find out," Candace said.

"But what if she says no, and it ruins our friendship? I'd be miserable."

"You mean, more miserable than you are now?" Tamara asked.

He sighed. "Why do women have to be so complicated?"

Candace tried not to laugh, but she couldn't help it. She had often wondered the exact same thing about men. She sat down next to him on the planter and patted his shoulder, feeling bad for laughing.

"Look, would you be happy just being friends with her forever?"

"No."

"Then you owe it to yourself—to both of you—to go for it. It's like taking off a Band-Aid. You can do it quickly and get it over with, or you can draw it out and let the pain go on and on. Which would you rather?"

He sighed. "I usually just wait until they fall off by themselves in the shower."

"Man," Tamara said, sitting down on his other side, "you can't just shower this away." She made a face as Candace giggled. "Just put everyone out of their misery and ask the girl out already."

Roger was nodding. "Okay," he said. Then he asked, "What should I get her for Christmas?"

"I'm sorry. I can't help you with that. I can't even help Candace figure out what to get Kurt for Christmas. You're on your own," Tamara said, standing abruptly.

Roger looked at Candace imploringly. "What do you think?"

"I think she'd love you forever if you gave her something chocolate, but I'd advise against it." Candace was joking, but a moment later she recoiled in horror as Roger leapt to his feet.

"That's it!" he shrieked. "Why didn't I think of that? Thanks!" Then he headed across the mall at a jog.

"Girl, what did you just do?"

Candace shook her head. "I'm a bad, bad person."

"Um, excuse me?"

Candace looked up. A nerdy-looking guy was standing there, twisting his hands in front of him and smiling sheepishly.

"What?" Candace asked.

"I need help figuring out what to buy for a girl."

Tamara rolled her eyes and grabbed Candace's hand. "I'm sorry, but that was her last client of the day. The love doctor is out."

Candace laughed as she let Tamara pull her along. "You've already done enough damage for today," Tamara said.

"Well, at least if I can't solve my problems, I can help someone else."

"I know. Let's forget Kurt, and you can help me."

"Help you figure out who to take to Winter Formal?"

"No, Lame-o," Tamara said. "Help me help you figure out what to get me for Christmas. I'm thinking maybe something ruby-ish this year."

"Oh no, uh-uh. This year I'm picking out a present for you by myself and I'm buying it myself."

Tamara looked nonplussed, and for a moment Candace thought she was going to argue with her. Finally, the other girl just shrugged. "Fine. Let's go get something for your mother or my mother, just as long as we *buy* something. I'm dying here."

Two hours later, Candace had gifts for her mother, father, and all four grandparents. Tamara had done similar damage but had also bought presents for extended members of her family that she usually exchanged with. They ended up at Rigatoni's for dinner, where they discussed what was left on their lists.

"I've got to get something for my friends at The Zone," Candace said. "I'm not even sure where to begin."

"Are we doing a gift exchange in that girls' Bible study you're going to be leading?" Tamara asked suddenly.

Candace blinked at her. She had barely thought about how she was going to lead the first meeting, let alone given any thought to a Christmas party or gift exchange.

Tamara waited for a moment and then said, "Okay, maybe a better question is whether there's even going to be an *idea* exchange at the first meeting, which is in two days."

"Don't remind me," Candace said with a sigh. "I should be home reading over the leaders' manual Pastor Bobby gave me."

"He gave you that two weeks ago," Tamara noted.

"Yes, thank you for pointing out my slacker ways in this area."

Tamara smirked. "Hey, at least I didn't let myself get roped into leadership."

"Duly noted. If you're not careful, though, I'll draft you."

"You'll try."

※

An hour later Candace was home in her room staring at the leadership manual. She had already hidden away her purchases, and she had no homework to distract herself with. There was just her and the manual and the slowly dawning realization that in two days, eleven other girls were going to be looking to her for guidance, thoughtfulness, and preparation.

"God, I'm not sure how I got myself into this situation, but please help me," she prayed. "Let me know what you want us to learn."

At least she didn't have to pick a topic. That was taken care of by Pastor Bobby. For eight weeks they would be studying the true meaning of Christmas. Every girl would have a workbook with each week's reading and questions all laid out for her. All Candace had to do was to facilitate the discussion and keep everyone on track.

Her mom entered the room, and Candace looked up. "Hey, Mom, what's up?

"I just wanted to remind you that tomorrow afternoon you promised you'd help me set up for Holly Daze."

"I remember. I'll be straight home after school, and we can go then."

"Thanks, I appreciate it," her mom said.

"Not a problem."

Her mom left the room, and Candace stared after her for a moment. Her mom was running one of the vendor booths in the Holiday Zone for Christmas. Well, technically, it was the organization her mom worked for that was in charge of the booth. They would be selling eco-friendly trinkets and spreading the word on environmental issues. Her mom and several others would work the booth.

It was weird thinking that she and her mom were going to be working at the same place, even if it was just for a few weeks. Since she was an elf, Candace's primary duties would also be in the Holiday Zone. Candance was relieved that her mom was coming into her workplace and not the other way around. As a vendor, her mom wouldn't have full referee privileges, which meant there were still a lot of places Candace could go in the park that her mom couldn't.

With a sigh she turned back to the book and jotted down a few notes. She looked at the twelve names on her list. There were three girls from each grade in her group. She recognized the names of all except two freshmen. The third, Jen, she had seen several times at youth group. She seemed like a nice girl, even if somewhat overwhelmed half the time.

Her Instant Messenger pinged, and she read the message from Josh.

> *Ready for D-Day?*
> **D-Day?**
> *Daze Day.*
> **More than U. Gotta help Mom set up vendor booth tomorrow.**
> *Kewl. Selling what?*
> **Eco-stuff.**
> *Stellar.*
> **Guess so.**

What U doing now?
Prepping for Bible study that starts Wed.
What on?
Christmas.
☺
☹ *I'm the leader.*
Not happy?
No. Don't know how well it will go.
Yule kill. Get it?
Haha.
Just be your elf.
You're in a good mood.
Luv Christmas.
What don't U luv?
Arbor Day. Don't tell your mom.
Gonna.
Snitch.
☺
OK. Gotta jet.
Later.

Candace smiled as she returned to the study. Josh always had a way of making her laugh. Now *he* would make a great Bible study leader. Actually, he would make a great leader of anything. He was passionate, funny, caring, and competitive. She sighed. It was too bad he and Tam wouldn't get together. She was sure they'd be great for each other.

With a sigh she closed the leadership manual. At least she had an idea of what was expected of her. She opened up the study and read the verses and then wrote down her answers to the seven questions. She might not be the world's best leader, but at least she could be prepared.

When she finished, she put the books away and rewarded herself with a phone call to Kurt.

"Hey, gorgeous," he said when he answered the phone.

She smiled. "Hey, yourself."

"Guess what I did today?"

"What?"

"I bought your Christmas present."

"What did you get me?"

"No way I'm telling you. Just know it's perfect."

Perfect. Instead of filling her with anticipation, the word filled her with terror. He thought he had gotten her something perfect, which meant that she had to find him something perfect. *No pressure*, she thought as she groaned inwardly.

"I've got my eye on something special for you," she fibbed. Maybe a little fishing would help her out.

"Like what?"

"Guess."

"A fishing pole and a mess of hand-tied flies?"

She actually pulled her phone away from her ear and stared at it for a moment, wondering in what spectacular way it was malfunctioning for her to have heard that.

"Um ... maybe," she said.

"Or how about one of those shower radios?" he asked.

"Are you wanting one of those?" she asked, trying to make her voice teasing.

"Not really, we've already got one."

"Well then, guess again," she said, her voice cracking a little.

"Ooooh, I know ... a set of wrenches."

She thought for a moment. He had to be playing her. She refused to believe that these were his best guesses at what she might think he would want. She took a deep breath. "You aren't really trying to guess, are you?"

"Of course not. I don't want to know what you get me. I want to be completely surprised."

"I see."

"It's fun playing, though. I mean, really, what would I do with more hand-tied flies?"

"Heaven only knows," she said, feeling nervous laughter coming on.

"Hey, what should I wear to Thanksgiving?"

"Just some Dockers and a button-down shirt would be fine," she said.

"I've got a tie."

"No, think a notch below church wear," she said without thinking.

"Okay," and his tone told volumes.

She winced. It sounded like he didn't know what church wear would be. "So, a tie would be too much," she hastened to say.

"You're sure?" he asked, now sounding thoroughly confused.

"Definitely."

"Okay. Well, I should go. I've got more studying to do."

"Okay, see you Thursday," she said.

"Yeah."

4

When Candace got home from school the next day, her mom had already loaded the van. After quickly changing into jeans and a T-shirt, Candace hopped into the van beside her mom.

"Ready to go!"

"Then let's get this party started," her mom said.

A few minutes later they reached The Zone. A large sign read, Welcome Holly Daze Vendors! and had an arrow pointing around the side of the park away from the player parking lot. After following several such signs, they parked in a referee-only area, where they found people unloading an assortment of vehicles. Referees were on hand, providing dollies and carts.

"It's going to be strange. It will be like we're working together," her mom said.

"Tell me about it," Candace said, jumping out.

"Need a hand?" Sue asked as she walked up, pushing a cart.

"Sure! What are you doing here? Were you pressed into service?"

Sue shook her head with a smile. "I volunteered. It beats cleaning bathrooms this afternoon."

"I guess it would," Candace's mom said as she came around the van. "Hi, I'm Patricia, Candace's mom."

"Pleased to meet you. I'm Sue."

"You were on Candace's team for that summer scavenger hunt, right?"

"The winning team," Candace pointed out with a smile.

They shook hands, and then the three of them set to work. Once they had loaded up the cart, Candace stared at how much was left in the van.

"It's going to take ten trips!"

"No, three," Sue said. "Trust me. I've been here all day."

They walked right into the Kids Zone, and Candace smiled when her mom gasped.

"I know, first time not going through the front gate is bizarre, huh?" Candace asked.

"And cool. I can see why you enjoy working here," her mom said.

From the Kids Zone they pushed the cart into the Holiday Zone. The noise and activity were nearly overwhelming. The area already had its Christmas overlay, which Candace hadn't seen yet. Lights and wreathes hung on every permanent structure in the area, and a giant tree illuminated the center. Booths were scattered all around for the outside vendors, and on hand was a small army of food carts to keep the busy vendors from getting too hungry or thirsty.

"Do you know what booth you're at?" Sue asked.

"Thirty-two."

"It's over there by the gingerbread house."

A giant gingerbread house dominated a maze in the center of the Kids Zone all year round. Although something seemed a little different to Candace, she didn't pay much attention until they stopped next to her mom's booth. Then she gasped. The usual house had been replaced by one made out of real gingerbread.

"That smells heavenly," Patricia commented.

"They just put it in this morning," Sue said. "It's real gingerbread, and even the glue that holds it together is made out of edible materials."

"You mean you could eat that thing?" Candace asked.

"Yeah. Someone probably will too."

"What do you mean?" Candace asked, her mind flying to Becca.

"One of the Game Masters told me they will be giving it away at the referee Christmas Party."

"Wouldn't that be something?" Patricia said.

"You've got a great view from your booth here," Sue said.

Candace looked at the booth. Like all the others it had about ten feet of counter space and a little awning to keep rain off. It was particularly well situated just to the right of the entrance to the maze.

"How about you start putting stuff where you want it, while Candace and I take care of emptying the van?" Sue suggested.

"Sounds like an excellent idea."

A few minutes later Candace and Sue headed back to the van with an empty cart.

"Your mom seems really nice," Sue said quietly.

"Yeah, she's pretty cool," Candace said. "She can be a bit tough, but that's okay."

"You're so lucky that you get to spend time with her."

"I take it you don't get much time with your mom?"

Sue shook her head and looked away.

They worked fast and had the cart loaded up again in five minutes. "I think you're right," Candace said as she closed up the van. "One more trip should do it."

"Told you," Sue said.

"So, how's college going?" Candace asked.

Sue smiled. "Piece of cake."

"Isn't it hard to juggle work and school?"

Sue shrugged. "It can be. The classes just haven't been that hard for me. I learned a lot of the stuff in high school, so most of it's really just a refresher."

"Bummer."

"Hey, at least I'm taking classes, and someday I'll get over to Cal State."

When they made it back to the booth, Candace was amazed at how much her mom had accomplished in such a short time. The antique-looking cash register sat proudly on a table next to two chairs. Merchandise was already sparkling on the green felt display areas. Her mom smiled at them as she hung an ornament from a hook on the roof of the booth.

"Special delivery," Sue called as they wheeled the cart to the back of the booth.

"I just don't know what it could be," Patricia said with an exaggerated smile.

The two laughed as they unloaded boxes, and Candace noticed how happy Sue looked.

After making a final run to the van, Patricia put Candace and Sue to work laying out merchandise on the counter and hanging wind chimes, ornaments, bird feeders, and art made of recycled material on the hooks.

"How did you decide to have a booth here?" Sue asked.

"The organization I work with chooses a venue each year to display holiday items and to attempt to raise awareness about environmental issues. This year we chose The Zone because of the excellent example it sets."

"How's that?" Sue asked.

"They recycle over eighty percent of all the materials used in the park."

"Well, then that means they're definitely eco-friendly," Candace said with a smile.

"Exactly," her mom said, giving her a quick hug.

It had always seemed somewhat funny to Candace that while she could speak easily with both her parents about their professions, she had never felt any desire to follow in either of their footsteps. It wasn't that she didn't care about justice or clean drinking water, but she just didn't feel like she had a passion for those things like her parents did.

Maybe someday she would find the thing that could make her talk for hours on a single subject to anyone who would listen. She hoped so. She envied them both their enthusiasm and dedication.

She shook her head. She was being too hard on herself.

More vendors arrived.

"I think we've monopolized you long enough," Patricia told Sue.

"Yeah, I need to go help cart things for other people," Sue said, sounding tired.

"Good luck with that," Candace said as the other girl took her cart and moved off.

"She's nice," Patricia said.

Candace nodded.

"She works janitorial, right?"

"Yeah, and she goes to the same community college as Kurt."

They worked for another hour, and when they were done, they stood back to admire their handiwork.

The booth looked inviting, and it blazed with color. It definitely outshone all the other booths that were finished. She gave her mom a quick hug.

"It looks amazing, Mom."

"Thanks. Thank you for all your hard work. I really appreciate it."

"No problem. You're not going to be the only one working it, are you?"

"No, there will be eight of us on rotation. I requested weekdays to work."

"Good for you. It's nice to have a choice," Candace said with a sigh.

"Not as much as I'd like. I'm working Friday."

"Looks like neither of us will be hitting the Black Friday sales," Candace said.

"Oh well, we'll just have to make up for it some other time."

Candace glanced at her watch. "What about now?" she asked.

"I think we could arrange for a banzai run at the mall," her mom said.

The run turned out to be a one-hour literal run. By the time it was done, Candace was exhausted but had gotten gifts for more than half the people on her list. She was still coming up with a huge blank, though, next to the name Kurt. There was a little nagging voice in the back of her head that said if Thursday didn't go well, she might just be crossing his name off her list. She shook her head. It was only Thanksgiving dinner, what could go wrong?

❄

Wednesday evening Candace was a bundle of nerves when Tamara came to pick her up for Bible study. She wasn't sure which she was more stressed out about: leading Bible study or the possibility of something going wrong with Kurt and her family in less than twenty-four hours.

"Are you sick?" Tamara asked suspiciously. "If you are, I'd appreciate you not giving it to me."

"I'm not sick, just stressed," Candace told her. "Just drive before I chicken out."

They arrived at the youth building to find the parking lot empty. "Maybe no one will show up," Candace said.

"Don't count on it. We're ten minutes early."

They walked into the building, and for one second Candace was filled with hope, until she saw a small figure sitting on one of the floor pillows, knees tucked under her chin. She recognized Jen.

"I'm so glad you're here!" Jen said. "I thought it was going to be just me."

"Candace was hoping it was just going to be her," Tamara said.

"Huh?" Jen asked.

"Nothing," Candace said, glaring at Tamara.

Candace and Tamara grabbed their favorite couch in the room, and Candace carefully laid out everything she was going to need. Her stomach was still twisting in knots.

Jen scooted closer. "I thought you were great in the maze at the Halloween thing at The Zone."

"Thanks," Candace said.

"It looked very exciting."

"A little too exciting," Tamara piped up.

Candace waved her hand. "Long story. Yes, I had fun, though. I'm glad you could come."

"Me too."

The other girls trickled in until they were all there. Everyone grabbed chairs and pillows and sprawled out in a rough circle. Finally, when everyone had settled in, they began.

"Hello and welcome to Bible study," Candace said.

The next hour seemed to fly by. The initial meeting was less about studying and more about getting to know each other and hearing each other's stories. Both Candace and Tamara were "pew babies" who had been born and raised in the church. There were other pew babies in the group, as well as several who had found Christ on their own or through friends within the last couple years.

It seemed like a good mix of girls, and Candace found herself relaxing as the time passed. Everyone there was eager to learn and discuss. That was going to make things a lot easier. She'd had nightmares where no one in the room talked except her.

When the study was over, Candace and Tamara headed to Big D's for ice cream, only to find that three of the other girls had the same idea. They all ended up at the same table.

"I can't believe tomorrow's Thanksgiving," Eilene said.

"I'm just so thankful for the four-day weekend. I'm totally exhausted," Rachel said.

"There's something we should talk about . . . what are we all thankful for?" Joy asked.

It was a logical question, one they could have discussed at Bible study. Candace just wished she had been the one to think of it. What was she thankful for? There was a lot. Good friends, family, God, The Zone—all were right up there.

"I'm thankful to live in a country where I'm free to say what I want and worship how I want," Eilene said.

Eilene's family had originally been from Poland, and even though Eilene had been just two when they came to America, she still cherished her freedom. It was nice. Candace took so many things for granted because she had never known anything else.

"I'm thankful that none of my teachers assigned homework for the break," Rachel said.

Candace smiled. Rachel could always be counted on to say something funny or lighthearted. She and Eilene were best friends. It seemed like such an odd combination, but they balanced each other out pretty well.

"I'm thankful for having the best friend in the whole world," Tamara said, smiling at Candace.

Tamara was sitting across the table, otherwise Candace would have hugged her. "VH," Candace said. *VH* was their code for Virtual Hug.

"VH back," Tamara said.

"What about you, Candace?" Joy asked.

"She's thankful she has a boyfriend to take to Winter Formal," Tamara teased.

Candace blushed. She hadn't even thought about Kurt. Too many thoughts crowded her mind. There were all the things she was thankful for and all the things she should be thankful for. Suddenly she wasn't in the mood to share, so she took the easy way out. "I'm thankful for ice cream," she said just as the waitress appeared with their order.

"I'm thankful to have a personal relationship with Christ Jesus," Joy said.

Of course you are, Candace thought. Joy was one of those girls who always gave the meaningful or pious answer. Candace could never tell if Joy really meant it or she just thought the show was expected.

"I think that one is a no-brainer," Candace said out loud and then clamped her hand over her mouth, horrified. *I so did not mean to say that out loud!*

Tamara laughed, and Eilene and Rachel joined in.

"At least it's something actually important, unlike ice cream," Joy said, a fake smile plastered across her face.

Now you've started a fight, good going. She sat there, a dozen retorts crossing her mind, and each of them more guaranteed than the last to inflame things. She decided to take a page from Rachel. "Yes, Christ is more important than ice cream. However, I believe that ice cream is clear evidence that God loves us and wants us to be happy," Candace said, smiling like a good elf should.

It worked. After a moment, Joy smiled back. "I can agree to that."

"I think we all can," Rachel added.

"Here, here," Tamara said, lifting a spoon.

Candace sighed to herself. Some days she had a real knack for getting on people's bad sides. She continued to smile at Joy as she dug into her ice-cream sundae. Only eleven more weeks of Bible study to go and then she could go back to sitting quietly in youth group and keep her big mouth from getting her into trouble.

5

Candace woke to the smell of turkey. She got up and ran downstairs in her pajamas just in time to see her father basting the bird.

"Good morning, sleepyhead," he said.

"It smells great!"

"It's coming along."

Her dad always cooked on holidays. He had been dubbed the "Grand Master of Thanksgiving" by friends and neighbors who had partaken of his Thanksgiving feasts.

On the back of the stove rose several loaves of yeast bread, and a bag of potatoes sat on the counter waiting to be peeled and chopped. Candace's stomach growled in anticipation.

"I need help with the table," her mom said as she passed by with linens in her arms.

"Just give me five minutes," Candace said as she dashed back upstairs.

Five minutes later she was back downstairs dressed in jeans and a tank top. She helped her mom set "the table" which was technically five tables: the dining table, the kitchen table, and three card tables all lined up end to end and stretching from the dining room through the living room.

They draped the tables with gold tablecloths before dragging folding chairs out of the garage to supplement the ten chairs that were normally around the dining room table. Candace picked up the piano bench and moved it to the foot of the table where two plates were squeezed together.

"Somehow I have a feeling you'll be volunteering to share the piano bench this year," her mom said with a smile.

"Well, Kurt and I could sit there," Candace said, feigning indifference, "if you wanted."

Once the chairs were arranged, they got out the china and silverware and laid out the place settings. As a final touch Candace folded orange and brown linen napkins for each place.

"Looks great!" her dad said as her mom set the cornucopia centerpiece in the middle of it all.

"Thanks," her mom said, surveying the layout. "Some day I'll have a dining room table long enough to seat all our guests," she sighed.

"Whoa! Time out. Last year all you wanted was matching chairs. Now you want a new table?" her dad teased.

"The longer I go with what I've got, the more I'm going to want," she said.

Candace smiled. They had been discussing the state of the seating arrangements every Thanksgiving for as long as she could remember.

"Well, I figure I just have to hold out a couple more years," her dad said. "Then Candace will be married and she can host Thanksgiving at her house. I'll be out of the woods on the whole table and chairs thing."

"What?" Candace asked, blushing uncontrollably.

"Candace is too young to get married," her mother said.

"I said in a couple of years," her father answered. "I don't expect Candace to get married today."

"Um, Candace is in the room," she said, trying to get her parents' attention.

"Yes, you are, honey," her mom said.

"So, I'm betting I know who thinks she's sharing the piano bench with a certain young man," her father said.

"Kurt and I are going to sit on the piano bench," Candace said.

"I remember when your mom and I sat on the piano bench together at her parents' house one Thanksgiving. You remember that, sweetheart?"

"No," her mom said, but the blush creeping across her cheekbones gave her away.

Candace bit back a giggle as she watched her dad make googly eyes at her mom. Her parents were the only ones she knew who could still act like teenagers when the mood took them. She just hoped she and her husband could be like that when they were older. *But not for a long time ... a very long time. Years even.*

Her dad turned his attention back to the table. "You know, I don't much like the color brown. Why don't we take off those napkins and put the green ones out?"

"Because green is not a Thanksgiving color," her mom said, shaking her head.

"Sure it is. Why, there are leaves on the tree that are still that color."

"The tree in the yard is green all year round," her mom pointed out.

"See? And orange—I really don't like orange. Red is a Thanksgiving color. Lots of leaves on the ground under other trees are red."

"So, let me get this straight. You want to take off the orange and brown and have the table be gold, red, and green?"

"Yes, why not?"

"Because those are Christmas colors," her mom said.

"Well, then let's have Christmas instead. I think I found where you hid my presents."

Candace doubled over laughing as her mom glared and wagged a finger at him. A timer went off in the kitchen, and he used it as an excuse to make his exit.

"Every year it's the same thing. We haven't even carved the Thanksgiving turkey, and he's trying to declare Christmas," her mom said.

"You love it, admit it," Candace said.

Her mom smiled. "Never where he could hear me."

By the time the first guests arrived, the house was spotless, the turkey was cooling, and Candace was dressed in black slacks and an emerald green blouse. Her dad had hugged her, tousled her red hair, and thanked her for bringing Christmas to the party even if her mom wouldn't.

Soon relatives and friends poured into the house bringing with them more sparkling cider than they could all drink in a week. Candace ended up with the job of grabbing the bottles at the door and stacking them in the garage to keep cool once they ran out of room in the refrigerator.

Each time the doorbell rang, her heart skipped a beat, because she thought it was Kurt. The more time that passed before his arrival, the more nervous she became.

The doorbell rang again as she was leaving the garage. "I'll get it!" she yelled, a little louder than she had intended.

She threw open the door and sagged in relief against it when she saw Kurt. He smiled at her nervously, and she suppressed the urge to giggle. He was wearing black Dockers and a green button-down shirt.

"Looks like I'm conforming to the dress code," he said with a tight smile.

She threw her arms around his neck and kissed him. Then, aware that others were watching, she quickly pulled away and stepped aside to let him enter.

"So that's the young man we've been hearing about," one of her mom's coworkers said, loud enough for Candace to hear.

"How sweet you two look with your matching outfits," her great-aunt Bernice exclaimed.

"Thank you, it was an accident," Candace said, vaguely feeling the need to explain.

"Then that means you're soul mates," one of her mom's other coworkers, the one Candace thought of as Hippie Freak, said with a dreamy-eyed expression.

The doorbell rang again, and Candace found herself in charge of four more bottles of sparkling cider—grape this time. She hurried them into the garage, feeling guilty about leaving Kurt alone for even a minute. She had just decided to take Kurt on a tour of the house when her mom called everyone to attention.

"Now that we're all here, you can go ahead and find a seat at the table," she said.

Candace grabbed Kurt's hand and dragged him over to the piano bench.

"What is this? The equivalent of the kid's table?" he joked as he tried to get his long legs under the table.

"No, dear. That's the lovers' bench," Bernice said, patting Kurt's hand as she sat down nearby.

"Meaning what, exactly?"

"Nothing," Candace said.

Bernice didn't take the hint. "It's the bench you sit on when you're in love. That piano bench has been in the family for generations, and every couple that shares a holiday meal sitting there is destined to get married."

"Destined?" Candace asked. This was the first she had heard of this particular family legend. She just wanted to sit really close to Kurt and feel like they were sharing something special.

"Married?" Kurt asked.

"Yessiree. Dozens. My late husband and I had Thanksgiving dinner sitting on that very piano bench in 1937."

"Bernice, you know that's just a silly superstition," Candace's mom called from halfway down the table.

"I believe it's true. Maybe the tree that gave its life for that piano was the reincarnation of an old village shaman or even a matchmaker," Hippie Freak chimed in.

"Reincarnation? Are you serious?" Kurt asked, turning to look at Candace.

"She is, but not me. I don't believe in reincarnation. Not at all. I believe you get one chance in this life to live, love, and accept Jesus Christ." Candace couldn't stop the words from tumbling out, and her voice got higher until she ended and realized that the entire room had gone quiet.

"And on that note," her dad said, "let's pray."

Everyone around the table reached out for the hands of the people on either side, and Candace grabbed Kurt's as she bowed her head and closed her eyes. She had held his hand dozens of times before, but it had never felt so awkward.

"Bless the cook and the cookin'. We're here to eat and not for lookin'. Amen."

There was laughter around the table, which helped ease the tension. Candace glanced up. Normally, her mom would have chastised her dad for teasing like that about grace, but even she was smiling.

"Seriously, Father God," her dad continued, "we thank you for these and all of life's blessings. We ask that you bless this food that it might be nourishing to our bodies. Amen."

"Amen," everyone chorused.

"Okay, grab the dish in front of you and pass to your left," her mom instructed.

"So, young man, what do you plan on doing with the rest of your life?" Bernice asked, leaning in close to Kurt.

Kurt's phone rang.

Saved by the bell, Candace thought.

He pulled his cell out of his pocket and looked at the display. "It's my roommate. I gotta take this." He extricated himself from the table, banging his knee on one of the legs and causing everyone's water glasses to slosh over. "Sorry."

He walked into the kitchen, and Candace could hear him talking.

"No, trust me, not a problem."

"That's right."

"I'll tell you later."

"See you in ten."

Her heart sank, and a moment later he walked back into the room, his face grim.

"Hey, Candace," he said, crouching down next to her. "My roommate's car broke down. I gotta go help him. I'm sorry."

"That's okay," she said. Maybe it was better this way. Dinner clearly had not been going well.

"You're the best," he said. He kissed her on the cheek be-fore standing up. "It was nice meeting everyone. Sorry I gotta run," he said with a wave.

Candace started to stand to let him out, but he was already at the door. He gave her a little wave and then was gone. Some-one handed her the bowl of mashed potatoes, and she piled some on her plate.

"Such a nice young man ... shame he had to leave," Bernice said.

"Yeah," Candace said as she passed her the potatoes. "He didn't even get to eat anything."

The only good thing about sitting alone on the piano bench was that she had a lot more elbow room than anyone else at the table. The rest of dinner went well. Her father had outdone himself, as usual.

After dinner everyone scattered to various parts of the house to visit and entertain themselves before dessert. Candace found herself in the kitchen, helping her mother load the dishwasher and put away the leftovers.

"I'm sorry Kurt had to leave," she said.

"Thanks," Candace replied with a sigh. "Not exactly the Thanksgiving I was picturing."

"You know, things rarely turn out like we'd want them to, but sometimes they can be wonderful in the most unexpected ways," her mother said.

"Are we talking about Thanksgiving or life?"

"Both," her mom said with a laugh. "But today, mostly Thanksgiving."

They finished up and joined the guests. A few minutes later the doorbell rang.

Candace jumped to her feet. Maybe Kurt was finished helping out his roommate and decided to come back. She opened the door to see a familiar figure, but it wasn't Kurt.

"Josh, what are you doing here?" she asked.

"Hey, I hope it's cool. The folks and I are done eating, and I thought I'd see if you wanted to catch a movie later. I tried your cell, but you weren't picking up. I decided to swing by, but it looks like you're pretty busy," he said with a sheepish grin. He ran a tan hand through his sandy hair.

"I'd love to go a little later. You want to come in?"

"If it's no trouble."

Candace's mom came over. "Hi, Josh, you know you're always welcome here."

"Thanks," he said, coming inside.

"You're just in time for pie too," she said. "I hope you've got room."

"There's always room for dessert," he answered.

"So, your family's already done for the day?" Candace asked.

"Yeah. Thanksgiving is the one holiday that's seriously low-key at our place. It's been that way ever since the 'Flaming Turkey Incident.'"

"That doesn't sound good."

"It wasn't. That sucker nearly burned down the house."

Candace laughed just thinking about it.

"And that wasn't the worst part."

"Oh no!"

"Oh yeah. Mom made us eat it."

"Yuck!"

"It was completely charcoal. It was so nasty."

"Next year you guys will have to come here then."

"It's a plan."

"Dessert time," Candace's mom called, and everyone reassembled at the table.

"You can sit next to Candace," her mom said, indicating the piano bench to Josh.

"Cool. A seat of honor."

Candace smiled as she squeezed next to Josh on the bench. Aunt Bernice looked at him in confusion for a moment and then said, "You're not the boy who was here earlier."

"No, ma'am, I just got here. My name's Josh. I'm one of Candy—Candace's friends," he said.

"Good to meet you," she said brightly.

Pie was passed out, and, as Josh and Candace ate the holiday dessert, she couldn't stop thinking about his mom and the flaming turkey. Her mom was right. Life didn't always turn out how you expected, and it wasn't the first time Josh had rescued a bad day for her. She smiled as she ate the pie.

6

It was still dark Friday morning when Candace arrived at the park. Tired referees stumbled into one another as they all assembled in the Holiday Zone. She and her mom had carpooled, and her mom patted her on the shoulder before heading for her booth.

Sue arrived and stood by Candace. "I can barely keep my eyes open."

"Tell me about it. I'm not sure how I'm going to get through the day. How was your Thanksgiving?"

Sue made a face. "I tried cooking a turkey, and it was a total disaster."

"Did you set it on fire?" Candace asked.

"No."

"Then it couldn't have been a *total* disaster."

Sue laughed. "That's true. I didn't set it on fire, it wasn't raw, and no one got food poisoning."

"Then it sounds like you did quite well." Candace laughed. She spotted Josh a few feet away and waved as he made his way toward them.

A ripple ran through the crowd, and Candace turned to see John Hanson, the owner of the park, standing on top of a box so that everyone could see him.

"He seems like such a nice guy," Sue said.

"He is. Really nice," Candace said, thinking about her previous meetings with him. "Hey, did you know that he's a Christian?"

"Sure. It's all over in his biography. I read it last year. I wasn't surprised."

"Many great theme-park founders, like Walt Disney and Walter Knott, were Christians," Josh commented, appearing beside her.

Candace nodded. She was going to have to get that book.

John Hanson raised his hand, and the crowd fell quiet.

"Well, it's Christmastime again. That means long hours, huge crowds, and eager children. We can make it through. I want you to enjoy the season. Christmas is a special time of the year, and each and every one of you has the opportunity to make it even more special for our players.

"Of course, I want it to be special for you too, which is why we have the annual Zone Christmas party. This year it will be on December twenty-second. Bring your family members for a great time.

"And, what would a party be at The Zone without a little friendly competition?" he asked, pausing to let referees shout and clap their hands.

"This year we have something a little different planned. Hidden somewhere in The Zone, somewhere only a referee can get to, is a golden candy cane. Whoever finds it will be the guest of honor at the Christmas party and will win prizes, gift certificates, and this life-size gingerbread house!" He waved his hand toward the gingerbread house in the middle of the maze.

A roar of approval went up from the gathered referees.

"So good luck, enjoy the season, and happy hunting."

"Wow! It's like the whole Willy-Wonka-golden-ticket thing," Sue said after the noise had died down and referees not working in the Holiday Zone began to disperse.

"Yeah, except there's only one candy cane," Josh said.

Candace could see Becca a little ways away, hopping from foot to foot in excitement.

"We better watch out for Becca," Candace said, mimicking something she had been told before she knew the other girl.

"I bet you Becca finds the golden candy cane," Josh said, following the direction of her stare.

"That's a bet I'm not taking. Of course Becca will be able to ferret out her key to sugar," Candace said.

"Gib looks worried," Josh said, referencing one of Becca's co-workers from the Muffin Mansion.

"He should be. We all should be," Sue said.

Martha, one of the supervisors, hopped up onto the box vacated by John, and someone handed her a bullhorn. "Okay, elves with me; everyone else scatter!"

"That's our cue," Sue said. "See you later."

As referees streamed out of the area, Candace saw John Hanson going booth to booth to shake hands with the various vendors. He stopped in front of her mom's booth. One of them must have said something funny, because they both burst out laughing.

Five minutes later Candace stood with the other elves in a cluster around Martha.

"Okay, ladies and gentlemen, this is the big leagues. Elf duty is difficult, challenging, and one of the most visible jobs that a referee can do. You'll be pushed to your limit daily. I need you to give one hundred percent to this job. Are you with me?"

Candace bobbed her head along with the others.

"Good. Now here's how it works. You'll be broken into four groups. Group A will handle line control. Those of you with previous line experience will fall into that category. Group B will get kids onto Santa's lap and off. Those with ride-loading experience will fall into this group. Group C will handle the prize disbursements. Those of you with vending experience will fall into this group. Group D will handle the photography merchandising. Those of you with store experience will fall into this group. Is there any one unaccounted for? No? Good.

"Group A, report to the front of the queuing area. Group B, congregate around Santa's chair. Group D to the merchandise booth. Group C with me."

Candace, Lisa, and half a dozen others followed Martha to the area just to the left of Santa's chair.

"Okay. During slow hours, only one of you will be working at a time, and you'll be on this side," Martha explained. "When it gets busy there'll be two of you, one on each side. Santa and the elves handling the kids are on the red carpet areas. You stay on the green carpet areas."

Candace looked down and saw where the carpet changed colors. That shouldn't be too difficult.

"This is very important," Martha stressed. "You stay on the green carpet. It's not your job to guard Santa. Group B is doing that. You're Group C. It's your job to guard the candy and the presents."

"Don't you mean distribute them?" one elf asked.

"I said *guard*, and I mean *guard*," Martha said with a cold stare. "You will also distribute, but don't forget to *guard*."

She picked up a basket filled with candy canes. "Every person who walks through here gets a candy cane—kids, teens, parents, whoever. Now, you will see here, behind the ropes, stacks of presents."

Candace looked, and, sure enough, there were dozens of presents wrapped in gold, silver, or candy cane paper. She didn't remember seeing anything like that when she was a kid.

"Now, presents are to be distributed sparingly—one or two an hour. Use your best judgment on who to give them to. Gold paper is a girl's gift, and silver paper is a boy's gift. Candy cane paper is generic. Gold girl, silver boy, candy generic. Got it?"

Candace nodded along with the others.

"Do not let the children or their parents bully, beg, or bribe you into giving out a present. If you have a problem, the red panic buttons are here on the underside of the candy-cane-striped rail behind you."

Candace craned her head to see the button. If her experiences at The Zone had taught her anything, it was that she was going to have to use that button at least once, and she wanted to be prepared for it.

"The last part of your job is to make sure that once everyone has received a candy cane, they keep moving down the ramp toward the merchandise booths. Keep the flow going. Otherwise the whole process comes to a halt, and kids have to wait three times as long to see Santa.

"So, today we have four people working from eight to four and four more working from four to midnight. Those of you who will be working tonight, get out of here and get some rest."

Candace, Lisa, and two other elves she didn't know were left.

"Okay, you four, because today is going to be a rough day, you're going to take turns. One hour here, then one hour walking around the park reminding kids to come see Santa. Got it? Okay. Lisa and Candace will take the first shift. First, though, we're going to go through a practice run. Lisa and Candace up; Laura and Chrissy on deck."

Lisa seemed rooted to her spot, so Candace crossed over to the other side of the stage area and took her place on the green carpet. She picked up the basket of candy canes and checked out the gift section.

Two loader elves moved onto the red carpet. Around the entire area she saw other elves taking up position. Then the man himself, Santa Claus, appeared. He majestically walked onto the stage and seated himself on his thronelike chair.

"Ready? Go!" Martha shouted, once more using the bullhorn.

Candace watched as excess elves, a few other referees, and some of the vendors were loaded into the queue area. They zigzagged through the maze of ropes until they came to a stop at the end of the line. An elf led one of the vendors by the hand over to Santa, and the vendor gingerly sat down on Santa's lap, laughing.

"What do you want for Christmas?" Santa asked.

"A Barbie doll ... for my daughter," the vendor hastened to add.

"Have you and she been good girls?"

"Yes."

"I'll see what I can do."

The second elf loader helped her off Santa's lap and sent her toward Lisa, while the first elf loader escorted another person up to Santa.

He asked the same questions, and then the vendor was headed Candace's way. She smiled, pulled a candy cane out of her basket, and handed it to the woman. "Have a Merry Christmas," she said.

"Thank you," the woman answered. "I'm Jewish, though."

"Happy Hanukkah," Candace said without missing a beat and remembering to smile.

They cycled through three more people each before Candace stepped aside to let Chrissy handle the distribution.

After about five more minutes, Martha shouted, "Nice work everyone. Remember, we're cycling in one-hour shifts today. Starters take your places."

"Good luck," Chrissy said as she handed the candy cane basket off to Candace.

"Thanks."

The extra elves and referees went about their business, and silence settled down on the area. Candace clutched her stomach, feeling nervous and a little sick as she battled the butterflies and waited for the opening of the park. She glanced over at Santa. He sat in his chair, appearing majestic and calm. For a moment she thought about asking him what she should get Kurt for Christmas. If anyone would know ...

She shook her head, laughing at herself. She was here to help Santa, not the other way around.

"Gates are open!" someone shouted.

Candace fidgeted with the handle of her basket. Any moment now it would begin.

"Incoming!"

A dozen kids with parents in tow ran through the ropes, shouting for Santa.

The first kid ran toward Lisa after shouting his requests to Santa at the top of his lungs. The next one was slightly more restrained, and Candace handed both him and his father a candy cane as they exited.

"I get to add sugar to this?" the father asked with a groan.

Candace just shrugged and smiled. "Merry Christmas."

The next dozen people didn't say a word to her; they just took the candy canes and dashed off.

A little girl climbed up onto Santa's knee, looked at him, and burst into tears. An elf picked her back up and gave her to her mother who apologetically herded the little girl toward Candace.

Candace felt so bad for her. She had probably been so excited to see Santa. Candace glanced at Santa and was surprised to see him staring at her. He gave a little nod.

"I didn't get to tell Santa what I want," the little girl sobbed.

Candace reached behind her and picked up a brightly colored package. *Gold for girl*, she mentally recited.

She bent down and handed the package to the little girl. "It's okay, honey, Santa knows what you want," she said.

"Thank you!" the girl said, clutching the present.

"Merry Christmas," Candace said, handing the mother a candy cane.

"Merry Christmas to you too," the mom said with an appreciative smile. "Come on, let's go."

The next hour flew by. When Chrissy relieved her, Candace was a little sad to leave her post. Candace left, though, and made a beeline for her mom's cart.

"I got a glimpse of you at work, and you looked great," her mom said.

"Thanks. I saw you laughing earlier with Mr. Hanson."

"Yes. I told him I was Candace's mother. He said he knew exactly who I was talking about, and we had a laugh. He's a very nice man and had some good things to say about you."

"I'm glad," Candace said. "Well, I gotta go make sure kids remember to come see Santa."

"Like they'd forget," her mom teased.

"Good luck with the selling," Candace said before taking off.

She spent the next hour walking around telling every kid she saw where to find Santa in the Holiday Zone. The best part was seeing the little crying girl again, this time clutching a doll.

"Thank you, Elf Candy!" the little girl shouted, waving.

Candace waved back.

"More like Eye Candy," Kurt joked.

Candace jumped. She hadn't seen Kurt walk up beside her. For some reason his comment irritated her.

"Hey," she said.

"Look, sorry I had to bail."

"No big. Is your roommate okay?"

"Yeah. We got his car fixed."

"Cool. Well, I gotta get back," Candace said.

"See you later."

"Yeah."

Candace walked away. She hadn't realized until that minute that she was mad at Kurt. She wasn't angry that he'd gone to help a friend. She was angry that he hadn't come back later or at least called. He could have come to the movies with her and Josh. She sighed. Why did romance have to be so complicated?

She made it back to her post only to find Lisa there looking miserable.

"What's going on?" she asked her.

"Laura quit."

"After an hour?" Candace asked incredulously.

"No. After five minutes."

"What happened?"

"You don't want to know. I wish I didn't know."

"Where's Chrissy?"

"When Laura quit, they moved her to the other side and closed this exit until Martha found me."

"Well, I'm here now. You can go."

"No, I have to relieve Chrissy."

Lisa moved away, misery showing in every line of her body. Candace wondered what on earth could have happened that could have been that bad. Then the first kid came flying at her, screaming for his candy cane, and she had no more time to think.

❄

On the way home, Candace and her mom barely spoke. It was four thirty and they were both completely exhausted.

"Sell much?" Candace finally asked when they turned onto their block.

"Thousand dollars worth."

"Cool."

"Yeah. You know your summer job?"

"Yeah?"

"I don't know how you kept it up."

It was a compliment. "Thanks."

They walked into the house and collapsed on the living room couch. The Christmas tree stood in its usual corner, already strung with lights. Boxes of ornaments littered the living room furniture and floor.

Her dad strode in, looking like the cat that swallowed the canary. "Well, the tree's ready for you," he said. "Lights are up outside the house too."

Candace wanted nothing more than to sleep, but the lure of sparkling lights and the desire not to break tradition propelled her to her feet. She grabbed up the first box of ornaments she could lay her hands on and headed to the tree with single-minded purpose.

"Of course, if you ladies would like some turkey sandwiches first, that could be arranged."

Candace immediately put the box down and headed for the kitchen.

7

After consuming leftovers, they all ended up back in the living room. Her dad turned on the stereo, and soon all the standard Christmas music was playing. Her mom started putting on the colored balls, while Candace went after the box of specialty ornaments. Her collection of stained-glass Rudolphs went up first, as she had to find a red bulb to put behind each of their noses. Next she hung the road runner ornament that was the very first ornament her parents had let her choose when she was a kid.

While she and her mom decorated the tree, her dad continued to string lights inside around the mantel and the ceiling. Exhausted as they all were, they found more things to laugh about than usual.

"Honey, did I tell you? The owner of The Zone has nice things to say about Candace," her mom said.

"Really? Well, you must be making quite an impression there to get his attention," her dad said. "Good for you. I knew you'd shine at whatever you chose to do."

"Seriously?" she asked, more than a little surprised.

"Of course. You're smart and talented. All you needed was a little challenge to bring out the best in you."

"Thanks."

"I like some of the friends you've made there too," her mom said. "Josh and Sue are particularly nice."

"I haven't met Sue, but Josh is a fine young man," her dad said.

Candace noticed that neither of them mentioned Kurt. She thought about saying something, but she was still angry with him herself.

"Sue's a year older than Candace, and she works in janitorial normally. She's very sweet and helpful. She seems sad, though."

"You know, I often think she looks a little sad, but I wasn't sure if that was my imagination," Candace said.

"I don't think so. She seems like she's suffered some kind of loss."

"I know she was planning on going away to college—Berkeley I think—but when I met her over the summer she said she was going to attend State because she needed to stay closer to home. Then a few weeks ago I saw her at the community college, and she told me she was there because it was cheaper than State."

"From U.C. Berkeley to community college? That is a change," her dad commented.

"So you really think there's something wrong?" Candace asked.

"It certainly sounds like it," her dad said. "People don't usually make those kinds of big changes without a reason."

"She has an air of tragedy about her," her mom added. "Poor thing. It's like she's so eager to say hi to me."

Candace remembered that Sue had said something about it being nice to talk with a mother. A sick feeling came over her. Was it possible that she had missed her friend's pain? Standing under the Christmas tree, she vowed that she would figure out what was wrong and do what she could to help. Sue was a great person and she deserved to be happy—especially at Christmas.

It was nearly midnight when they finished with the decorations. They turned off all the interior lights and enjoyed the Christmas lights for a few minutes before calling it a night.

Upstairs in her room, Candace saw that she had a message from Kurt. "Hey, Candace, I just wanted to call and apologize again for yesterday. It took a long time to fix his car, and I was in a bad mood afterward. I should have called but I didn't, and I'm sorry about that. Call me back and let me know everything's okay."

She called him back and he answered, sounding like she had awakened him.

"Are we cool?" he asked.

"We're cool," she said.

They said good night, and she got ready for bed. At least when Kurt upset her, he seemed to take responsibility for it. She would rather he had called her the night before, but at least he had called now. She climbed into bed and crushed Mr. Huggles, her stuffed bear, to her chest as she prayed.

❄

Saturday morning when her alarm went off, Candace briefly considered tossing it across the room. She was at least some- what gratified when she encountered her mom in the kitchen a few minutes later looking bleary-eyed herself.

"Morning," Candace said.

Her mom grunted as she sipped her coffee. A few minutes later when they headed out to the car she finally spoke. "I'm re- ally glad I'm not working tomorrow."

Candace smiled grimly. "Lucky you."

They arrived at the park, and her mom made a beeline for her booth. Candace took her time and admired all the Christmas decorations as she walked. Not only was the Holiday Zone decorated, but several of the rides had special seasonal overlays. The ride where players controlled the spin of their vehicle on a large disc-shaped surface had been completely transformed so it looked like they were riding in giant round Christmas ornaments. The tall slide had been themed to look like a giant toboggan ride. Even the theater where Freddie McFly and the Swamp Swingers and Mr. Nine Lives, the Daredevil Cat, entertained daily had a holiday-themed show, which included Mr. Nine Lives on ice skates. It was exciting to be a part of it all, and she had a sneaking suspicion that Christmas would be her favorite time of year to work at The Zone.

Finally, she walked over and took her place with the candy canes and presents. She waved to Chrissy, who was already on her side of the exhibit with her basket of candy canes in hand. A minute later Christmas music started playing throughout the area. Candace didn't remember hearing it the day before. She wasn't sure if the noise from the kids blocked it out or if someone had forgotten to turn it on.

As if the music was his cue, Santa walked onto the stage and took his seat. The first kids hit the area, screaming as they came. Candace smiled. So far this was the best job she'd had at the park, and she couldn't figure out why on earth they were giving her hazard pay for it.

It only took a couple of minutes to realize that it was going to be a lot busier day than the one before. By the time the park had been open for an hour, the line to see Santa was a two-hour wait. After another hour it was even longer. An elf named Ann came to give her a morning break, and Candace hurried off field.

Ten minutes later she was back on field, heading back to the Holiday Zone. At the railroad tracks, she slowed by habit and turned to see where the train was.

It was quite a way down the track, but still she hesitated. Pete, also known as Crazy Train Guy, had a habit of trying to run over referees. Although they had kind of become friends, she couldn't trust that to save her.

"It's safe to cross."

Candace looked and saw Josh standing on the other side of the tracks. "Are you sure?"

"Yeah. He almost never tries to kill anyone during Christmas."

Candace stepped forward, and, sure enough, the train didn't accelerate in her direction. She crossed to the other side.

"Good to know," she said.

A few seconds later the train passed by. It, too, got a complete Christmas overlay and became the Train to Santa's Workshop. Pete sat inside the engine, a Santa hat cocked to one side of his head in a crazy fashion that for some reason made Candace think of a devil with only one horn. He smiled and waved at her, and, surprised, she waved back.

"See? He loves Christmas. At Christmas everyone loves trains."

"Oh, so that's the secret. Cool." She turned and got a really good look at Josh. At first glance, he looked like an elf dressed all in red and green. However, none of the elves wore lederhosen.

"So, what exactly is your job?" Candace asked, looking over Josh's outfit.

"I'm a cheermeister."

He fell into step with her as she walked back to her position.

"Okay. That's a new one. What's a cheermeister? I hope it's not like a cheerleader, because I'm not sure you'd look good in the skirt."

"I have great legs, thank you very much."

She rolled her eyes at him. "Seriously, cheermeister?"

"It's the best job in the park. I get to make sure everyone's having a good time."

"And just how do you do that?"

"I look for problems, and I fix them. Kid drops an ice-cream cone on the ground, and I get him a new one. If players lose something in the park, I help them find or replace it. Occasionally, I get to give out cool gifts too, like complimentary dinners and free merchandise."

"So, like me with the candy canes and presents, but on a park-wide scale?" Candace asked as they arrived back at her station and Ann surrendered the candy cane basket.

"Exactly. We work to bring cheer."

"So how far ahead did you have to apply to be a cheermeister?"

"March."

She threw a candy cane at his head. He caught it and grinned. "I'll put this to good use."

"Cheermeister!" a little boy shrieked, running forward and wrapping his arms around Josh's legs.

"See? Everyone loves the cheermeister," Josh said as he bent down and plucked a present from the stack behind Candace and handed it to the little boy.

"Hey! Those are my presents," Candace protested.

Josh grinned. "Cheermeister. I trump. Well, I gotta go."

He waved to all the kids in line, and they waved back.

Candace shook her head and turned to give the next child down the ramp a candy cane. The father, who looked tired, waved the candy cane away. Candace just kept smiling.

She turned and saw the next child go flying in Chrissy's direction, while a boy who was probably about eight sat down on Santa's lap and grabbed him by the beard, jerking on it repeatedly while rattling off his list of demands.

What a horrible child! Candace thought, glancing over at the father who seemed indifferent to his son's behavior. Next to him stood another boy who looked just as determined to tell Santa what he wanted.

Santa did his best to extricate his beard, and the elves rushed to help him. That was when it happened. The second boy sprang forward, swerving away from Santa, and headed straight toward Candace. She stepped back so that he could get by her, but he turned and plowed into her, knocking her backward. Her hair wreath went flying. She tottered, trying to regain her balance, and he swooped down and grabbed two gold presents from her stack. She reached down to stop him, and that's when his brother hit her broadside.

She landed on her arm and knee, and pain seared through her leg as she struggled to get up. She heard something tearing. The older brother had also gotten his hands on two gold presents by the time Candace was able to reach for the panic button. Before she could push it, she saw security guards rushing toward them. She could see children in line struggling against their parents, and three of them finally broke away and ran toward her.

She craned her head around and saw that the elves had gotten Santa out of sight. As she looked back at the kids, she could hear Martha's warning about guarding the presents and smiling. She rolled over until the presents were wedged against her back. The hard edges dug into her. *They'll have to come through me to get to them*, she thought.

The father of the two monster children had joined them in running away. The first security guard reached her at the same time the three kids did, and the guard swooped, tucking a child under each arm, and ran with them back toward the line. The third child fell upon Candace, beating her with tiny fists and screaming, "Present!" at the top of his lungs. He stepped on her fingers, and one fist caught her on the cheek. Pain seared through her.

The second security guard grabbed him and headed over to assist his partner with crowd control. Candace pointed toward the fleeing father and children, and two more security guards took off after them.

The fifth security guard knelt down beside her. "It's okay, Candace, you can stop smiling," he said.

"Thank you," she whispered.

"How bad are you hurt?" he asked.

She shook her head. All she knew was that there was pain everywhere.

"I need a stretcher for one of the candy cane elves," he said, speaking into his radio.

A garbled reply came back.

"Yes, it's Candace," he answered.

Of course it's Candace, she thought as she laid her head down. *Who else would it be?* Not a season could go by that she didn't find herself in "the Hospital Zone."

8

The stretcher arrived, complete with a paramedic, her mom, and Josh. "This is weird," Candace said as she stared up at all of them.

Pain was knifing through her left knee, growing increasingly worse by the minute. The guard said something about the shock wearing off. He also kept her from looking at her leg, which was starting to freak her out.

"Oh my!" her mom burst out when she saw Candace.

Josh went completely pale. "Hey," he said, his voice shaking. "I heard someone over here needed a cheermeister."

Suddenly a wave of pain unlike anything she had ever experienced before washed over her, and all she could do was scream. It ended a few seconds later. "I'm sorry!" she gasped. "I couldn't help it."

Another wave of pain came and she screamed again. It felt like fire was pouring through her body. The wave stopped, and she felt herself slump.

She saw Lisa appear behind the others. "Only Candy can scream that loud," she was telling someone.

"Your knee is dislocated," the paramedic explained. "You're going to continue to have waves of pain like that until it's put back in. Normally, I'd wait until we had you in the nurse's station, but it's going to be a long, bumpy ride on this stretcher and—"

Candace screamed again as another wave hit her, and she couldn't hear what he said next. "I'm sorry," she gasped again when it was over. "Can you fix it?"

"Yes. I've seen a couple of these before, but it's going to hurt." He turned and addressed himself to the others, "You might want to look away."

Josh knelt down next to her head and started stroking her hair. He looked like he was going to be sick.

"Don't throw up on me," Candace warned.

"I won't," he promised.

The paramedic and the guard moved her onto her back, and another wave of pain had her screaming for what seemed like forever.

"That famous Candy scream. People all over the park will know it's you," Josh said.

Her left leg was bent, and she felt the guard grab her foot. "Pull her leg straight slowly," the paramedic said.

When her leg was nearly straight, she felt the paramedic touch her kneecap and shove it back into place. The relief was instantaneous.

"Thank you!"

"It's going to be incredibly sore, and you'll have pain for a few days, but at least everything is where it should be," the paramedic said.

He and the guard lifted her up and put her on the stretcher.

"The evil little boys took girl presents," she said. Somehow that made it a little better. They weren't likely to like what they got.

"We'll find them," the guard assured her.

"You two can come with us," the paramedic said to her mom and Josh.

"What about your booth?" Candace asked.

"Sue's watching it for me," her mom said.

Things started to get a little fuzzy, so Candace closed her eyes and let herself drift.

A few minutes later they arrived at the nurse's station, and the paramedics placed her on a bed. She opened her eyes and saw the kindly nurse who always seemed to be there.

"Hi," Candace said.

"I heard there was an elf down, and somehow I just knew it had to be you," the nurse said, shaking her head.

"I had to come see 'the Hospital Zone,' " Candace said with a smile. "Can we have a ceremony renaming this place just like we did for the Party Zone over the summer?" she asked.

"Sure, why not."

A minute later one of the other security guards came in with a bandage wrapped around his hand.

"And what happened to you?" the nurse asked.

"We got the family who attacked the candy cane elf, and one of the boys bit me. I just want you to check me for rabies."

"You caught them?" Candace asked.

"Yes. They've been ejected from the park."

"What about the presents?"

"They had already abandoned them. Luckily, we found them and gave them to a family with four little girls."

Candace smiled.

"All right, you take that bed over there," the nurse said, directing the guy with the bite. "Everyone else, into the waiting room while I assess the damage."

Candace waved to Josh and her mom as they headed reluctantly out of the room.

The nurse took five minutes to clean and bandage the guard's hand before turning her attention to Candace. She gave her some pain killers. "Your tights are ruined," she said, producing a pair of scissors and finishing the job of cutting them away. The nurse then gave her a thorough examination.

"Well, you've got a lot of cuts and bruises, especially on your shoulder. You're going to feel those for a while. And you're going to have a nasty bruise on your cheek. What happened there?"

"One of the other kids hit me, trying to snag a present."

"Nasty business."

"What about my knee?"

"You need your own doctor to check it out, maybe do a couple X-rays. It's likely he'll put you in physical therapy to strengthen the muscles around the knee, just to make sure the kneecap doesn't try to slip back out. Other than that, you're going to have to keep it pretty immobile for the next few weeks."

Candace blinked at her. "What do you mean by immobile?"

"I mean this," the nurse said, bringing out a full leg brace and a pair of crutches.

"How am I supposed to work in that?" Candace asked.

"Oh, I think that's the least of your worries," the nurse said.

"How am I supposed to go to Winter Formal in that?"

"Carefully. Now let me show you how to put it on. Then someone needs to take you home to get some rest."

The brace went all the way from her ankle to her hip and prevented her from bending her knee at all. Once it was on, Candace struggled to swing her leg off the bed, stepping with her right foot first and then swinging her left leg after.

"How am I supposed to use the crutches if I can't bend my leg?" she asked.

"At first you'll shift your body so your left hip is higher in the air than your right one. Don't worry, though, you should be able to put weight on it Monday, after you see your doctor. Then you'll just use the crutches for balance and support."

Candace felt her head start to spin, and she grabbed onto the bed for support.

"I gave you some pretty potent painkillers, and I'll send some more home with you. They'll likely make you sleepy and a little dizzy. " She grabbed a wheelchair, and Candace collapsed into it gratefully, although she struggled just to do that without being able to bend her left leg.

The nurse wheeled her into the waiting room, and her mom and Josh rushed forward.

"She should see her doctor on Monday," the nurse said to her mom. "He might want to set up some physical therapy for her knee. She'll need to wear the brace for the next couple of weeks, even while she's sleeping, to make sure the muscles around the kneecap can heal," the nurse said. She handed Candace's mom a small bottle of pain killers. "She can have one of these every six hours ... no more." Next she handed Candace's mom the crutches.

"Well, let's get you home," her mom said.

Josh grabbed the handles on the back of the wheelchair. "Lead the way," he told her mom.

They exited the nurse's station, and Candace was shocked to find dozens of referees outside. When they saw her, they began to clap and cheer.

"What's going on?" Candace asked.

"It's already spreading around the park how you sacrificed your own body to save the presents," Josh said.

"I'm not sure it happened exactly like that," she said.

"Just wait, by tomorrow you'll have saved Santa Claus and Christmas," he joked.

She had to laugh. "What am I? The center of all urban legends that surround The Zone?"

"It would seem so," her mother said. "All morning referees have been asking me if I'm the mother of Candy who was trapped in the park with a psycho killer over the summer."

Candace shook her head, but the action made her even dizzier.

"Wave to your fans," Josh said.

She waved and smiled lopsidedly, and everyone cheered louder. Several fell in behind them and walked with them across the park.

"I feel like I'm in a parade," her mom said.

"Welcome to The Zone, where anything can and will happen," Candace said.

Everyone they passed—even players—cheered and waved at her, although Candace was sure none of them knew why. She just kept waving back with her good arm. Even through the pain medication, she could feel the throbbing in the shoulder that had hit the ground.

At last they rolled off field and were soon at her mom's car. After a brief discussion, her mom and Josh decided it would be better if she rode home in the backseat so that she could put her leg straight out. Her mom opened the back door on the driver's side, and Josh helped her stand up and swivel around until she could sit on the seat. She then used her good foot and arm to push and drag herself backward until her back was against the far door and her legs were stretched out. Her mom came around the other side and helped her fasten the seat belt.

They closed the doors, and Candace leaned her head back against the window and sighed. What a mess. She didn't know why this had happened to her. *God, I have no idea what you're saying with this, but it better not have anything to do with Winter Formal.*

Josh and her mom were talking about something, but Candace was too tired to try and hear what it was. Finally her mom got in the car.

"You okay back there?"

"Yeah."

"Let's get you home."

Candace dozed off. She woke up when her mom parked in their driveway. She wondered how she was going to find the strength to get herself back out of the car without hurting her leg or her shoulder.

Her father came out, though, as soon as the car was parked. Apparently, her mom had called him sometime during the drive.

He opened the back door and said, "Put your good arm around my neck."

She did, and he put an arm around her back and another under her legs and half dragged–half lifted her out of the car. Once she was free, she expected him to put her down, but instead he carried her into the house and set her on the couch.

A moment later her mom followed with the crutches, which she placed nearby before positioning pillows to make Candace comfortable. "Would you rather go to bed?" she asked.

Candace shook her head. "I'd like to watch some Christmas movies," she said.

Neither of her parents seemed surprised. Her dad started the Albert Finney version of *A Christmas Carol* for her, and then her parents moved into the kitchen to talk. Candace struggled for a few minutes to stay awake but finally drifted off.

Pain woke her up just after four o'clock. After helping her manage a bathroom run, her mom gave her some stew and then let her take another pain killer. When the pain began to ease, Candace thought about going back to sleep, but she was more alert and feeling a little restless.

"Anyone want to play a game?" she asked.

The doorbell rang before either of her parents could answer. A moment later her mom announced, "Candace, you have visitors."

Candace struggled and managed to sit up a little straighter as she turned to look. Sue and Becca waved as they came to-ward her.

"Hi! What are you two doing here?" Candace asked.

"Josh is organizing the visiting parties," Sue said with a smile. "He's staggered it so we're all coming in shifts over the next day and a half."

Candace smiled. "We just got off work," Becca explained.

"I can only stay a little while," Sue said.

"But I'm here until the next shift," Becca grinned.

"You don't have to do this," Candace protested.

"Yes we do. We're here to entertain the fallen hero," Sue laughed.

"Can I offer you ladies some stew?" Candace's mom asked.

"Yes, please," they chorused.

A minute later Sue and Becca were eating and trying to talk at the same time. "You keep this up, and they're going to erect some sort of statue to you," Becca finally said.

"What, most injured referee in park history?"

"Nope, most heroic," Sue said.

Candace rolled her eyes. "Please."

"First psycho killers and now child mobs," Becca replied.

They chatted for a few more minutes before Sue stood up. "I have to get home," she said.

"Would you take some stew with you?" Candace's mom asked.

Sue hesitated for only a moment before nodding vigorously. "Everything went well at the booth, by the way. I sold fifteen hundred dollars worth of merchandise before your replacement showed up," she said.

"Wow! I should have you work the booth every day."

Sue took a disposable container filled with stew and then turned to Candace. "Feel better soon."

"Thanks. I'll try," Candace answered.

Once she had gone, Becca leaned forward conspiratorially. "Do you know a guy at your school named Brad Miller?"

"Yeah. He's in a couple of my classes. Why?"

"He asked me to go to your Winter Formal with him."

"Wow, what did you say?"

"Yes."

"What about Roger?" Candace asked.

Becca shrugged. "What about him? He's never asked me out."

"He wants to," Candace said.

"Wanting to and actually doing are two different things. So, do you know much about Brad?"

"He seems like a nice guy. How do you know him?"

"He worked in the Exploration Zone over the summer. He came by the Muffin Mansion earlier this week to ask me to the dance."

"Well, that'll be fun. We'll see each other there."

Becca looked at Candace's leg brace.

"I'm going with or without this thing," Candace said.

"Good. I'm going to need a friend there in case he turns out to be a jerk."

Becca left a couple hours later when Kurt showed up. "How are you doing?" he asked, wincing as he looked at her bruised cheek.

"Okay," she said.

"Looks like once again you were in trouble and I wasn't there to rescue you," he said, his face brooding.

"Don't worry about it. You're there for me lots of times. Besides, you can't follow me around the park. It's not your job," she said, smiling in an attempt to get him to smile back.

It didn't work. He just frowned more deeply. "If it was my job, I'd have been fired by now."

"Hey, who's cheering who up?" she asked. Her shoulder was throbbing, and she wasn't in the mood to make him feel better.

"Sorry. Guess I'm pretty much a loser all the way around."

Candace closed her eyes and tried to quash the irritation that was rising within her. This was so not about him. She couldn't think of any way she could salvage the situation, and she was really too tired to try. Fortunately, her mom saved the day.

"Candace, honey, it's been a big day, and you're looking pretty pale. I think maybe you should try to get some sleep."

"Yeah. I'll go so you can do that," Kurt said, jumping quickly to his feet.

"Thanks for coming," Candace said.

"No problem."

Seconds later he was gone.

"You scared him off," Candace tried to joke.

Her mom shook her head. "That one scares himself. Now let's get you to bed."

Candace couldn't agree more.

9

On Sunday morning, the first visitors arrived at ten in the morning. Roger and Martha were both smiling as they walked into the living room. Roger handed Candace her hair wreath, which she had lost the day before.

"They found it buried in the present pile," he said.

"Thanks," she said with a smile. "Now, I just need to get new red tights and have my costume cleaned."

"I wouldn't worry too much about that," Martha said with a smile. "We'll be moving you off elf duty."

"What? Why?"

"Well, you remember, it's company policy that referees get moved to other duties while accidents are investigated."

Candace sat up straighter. "That made sense at Halloween when that board was loose, but this is totally different. This wasn't an accident. There's nothing to investigate. I want to go back on elf duty as soon as my doctor says it's okay."

"Why on earth would you want to do that?" Martha asked.

"I think I know," Roger said, smiling at Candace. "If you don't get right back on the horse, you never will."

"That's right. This isn't the first time I've gotten hurt, but it's the first time I was attacked by a bunch of kids. I don't want to live in fear of children for the rest of my life."

"Yeah," Roger added, "you don't want her to have such issues with kids that she never has children because of it."

Candace looked at Roger, checking to see if he had lost his mind. His argument, though, seemed to be persuasive to Martha.

"I can see your point. Let me see what I can do about this."

"Thank you," Candace said.

"Now, let's talk about something else. Roger, have you finally asked out Becca?" Martha asked.

"You know that I like her?"

"Everyone knows, dear."

"No," Roger said. "Worse, someone's asked her out to a dance at Candace's school."

"Then I suggest you find a way to go to that dance and sweep her off her feet," Martha said.

Roger turned and stared at Candace.

"Don't look at me. I'm taking Kurt."

Roger sighed in misery, and Candace couldn't help but feel sorry for him.

When Roger and Martha finally left, Pete and Gib arrived to take their place. Neither was as talkative as Roger or Martha, but they both played a mean game of Trivial Pursuit, and Candace found herself enjoying their company.

After they finally left, she had an hour to herself before Josh and Tamara arrived. She must have been dozing, because she suddenly heard Tamara say, "Enough with the cheermeister!"

"You can never have enough cheermeister," Josh said, as the two of them walked into the living room.

Tamara rushed over, and when she realized that hugging Candace could be painful, she awkwardly patted her head instead.

"Hey, Candace, looking better than yesterday," Josh said with a grin.

"You two didn't drive over together, did you?" Candace asked.

"And I'll be regretting it for years," Tamara said with a snort of disgust.

Candace smiled. "So did the cheermeister bring me something?"

"I did," Josh said brightly, handing her a pillow shaped like a candy cane that he'd been hiding behind his back.

"I told him you'd beat him with that thing when you're feeling better," Tamara said. "I brought you something practical."

"Ice cream?" Candace guessed.

"Natch."

Tamara produced two pints of Ben and Jerry's ice cream. One was fudge brownie and the other was cookie dough. The banter went on, and Candace tried not to laugh too hard—she didn't want to hurt herself. They both stayed for dinner and finally left when Candace was ready for sleep again.

❄

On Monday, Candace and her mom went to the doctor to have her leg checked out. It was Candace's first real opportunity to use the crutches as she hobbled into his office, panting from the effort. After taking an X-ray, he reiterated what The Zone nurse had already told her and set another appointment in two weeks. He also said that as long as she stayed on the crutches, she could go back to school and work as soon as she was ready.

Once they made it back home, Candace called Martha to update her. Martha said that she had discussed it with her bosses, and they were willing to let Candace return to work the following Monday.

As soon as school was out, Tamara came over and brought Candace her books and a get-well card created by the drama class.

"Your legend grows at school," Tamara said humorously as she sat down in one of the chairs.

"How so?" Candace asked with a groan.

"Apparently, you're a hero. You were run over by an out-of-control mob, and you rescued some little girl, and gave toys to dozens of needy kids."

"What little girl?" Candace asked, bewildered.

Tamara shrugged. "I did manage to track the stories down to a guy named Brad. You know him?"

"No, but apparently he worked at The Zone over the summer, and he's taking Becca to Winter Formal."

"Roger must be heartsick," Tamara said.

"Speaking of heartsick. How's Mark?" Candace asked.

Tamara rolled her eyes. "I had to tell him to back off, that I was definitely not going to go out with him again."

"I'm sure that did loads of good for his ego," Candace said.

"There's only so much I'm willing to do for my cousin. I think he'll be okay, though. I was a lot nicer to him than that just sounded."

"Glad to hear it."

"So, do you need help prepping for Wednesday night, or are you even going?"

"Wednesday night?" Candace asked, at a momentary loss.

"Hellooo, Bible study. Remember?"

"I totally forgot."

"No, really? I mean, I guess considering the circumstances no one would blame you if you stepped down. Joy would probably love to take your place," Tamara said with a smirk.

"That's not going to happen," Candace said.

"A little territorial?"

"Are you antagonizing me on purpose?" Candace asked in disbelief.

"Of course. I really don't want Joy leading the study. I figure if I push your buttons you'll step up."

"Since when does that work?"

"Oh, I don't know. Are you going back to being an elf?"

"On Monday."

"Then it's worked since you started working at The Zone."

Candace stared at her for a minute. "Seriously?"

"Seriously. Don't get me wrong, I think it's a good thing. You're much more likely to stand up for yourself and fight for what you want now. I respect that."

"Yeah, but that implies that I want to lead this Bible study."

"Don't you?"

Candace hesitated. A week before, she would have said no, absolutely not. Now, if she was being honest with herself, she realized she did want to lead it. The first week hadn't been all that bad, but she also knew she could make it better. She laid her head back against a pillow and groaned.

"Knew it," Tamara said, and Candace could hear the smugness in her voice.

"Can you get me the study book and my Bible from upstairs?" Candace asked.

❄

On Wednesday night, Tamara pushed the passenger seat in her car as far back as it could go so that Candace could ride in the front. It was a tight fit, but she made it and felt triumph in the victory. Unlike the week before, she actually felt prepared, and she had found herself looking forward to the Bible study all day. She was also using it as a bit of a test run. Her parents had told her that they would leave the decision of when to go back to school up to her as long as she went back there before going to work. She figured if she could make it through the study, she would try school in the morning.

When they arrived at the youth building, Tamara carried her stuff while Candace hobbled in on her crutches. She knew she looked pathetic. The bruise on her cheek was deep purple. There were bruises and scratches on her good leg and on both arms, but the majority of her pain radiated from her injured shoulder. It made walking with the crutches that much more difficult.

She sat down on the couch and, at Tamara's insistence, put her leg up. Tamara dragged a chair over so she could sit next to her. Everyone else was already there and quickly formed a circle, staring openly at the brace on her leg.

"I got hurt at work," Candace started.

"We know," Jen spoke up.

"Oh, okay. Well, then let's start."

The focus of the Bible study was on spiritual journeys. They compared themselves to the wise men and shared how their "walk with God" was going. She asked the group members to pinpoint an area of their lives where they knew they had grown over the previous year.

"I used to smoke and I've quit, mostly. I still backslide some, though," one of the girls admitted.

Candace couldn't relate, but she nodded encouragingly.

"Every time I try to pray I fall asleep," Jen said with a heart-felt sigh.

"That happens to me too," said Tamara.

"Really?" said Jen.

"I think most of us have been there," Candace said. "It's one of the hazards of praying at night in bed."

Candace scanned her notes briefly. "So, I have a question. Is everyone happy with where they are on their spiritual journey?"

Each one of them shook their head no.

"Well, then I was thinking we should try this week to find one thing we can do to further our growth."

There was silence for a minute, and Candace held her breath, not sure if everyone was going to get on board with the idea.

"Like how can I not fall asleep when praying?" Jen asked.

"Exactly," Candace said, relieved at the example.

All around the circle heads began to nod.

When the study was done, Candace struggled back to Tamara's car and settled in, happy with how things had gone. Even Joy had seemed to be on the same page.

"You realize what you've done?" Tamara asked as she started the car.

"What?"

"You and I also have to find a way to grow this week."

"You've discovered the fatal flaw in my otherwise brilliant plan."

"I don't mind you being tough on yourself, but next time can you leave me out of it?" Tamara complained, but her tone was lighthearted.

"Next time, no growth for you."

"That's the spirit. So, you going to school tomorrow?"

"I guess. Can I count that as my growth moment?"

"Not even."

❄

School the next day took so much out of Candace that her parents urged her to stay home Friday. She went anyway, and it went better than the day before. All weekend she alternated between resting on the couch and practicing on the crutches until she had more confidence. On Sunday after church, Josh brought her a pair of new tights from the costume department, and her mom made sure her costume was in good shape. Monday at school went a lot better, and she headed over to The Zone in the afternoon, tired but ready to get back to work.

She gave herself plenty of time to get there. Her muscles were so tense they vibrated, but she refused to let it get to her. The attack had been a fluke. She was going to be fine.

Once in the Holiday Zone, she had some time to kill before her shift started. She hadn't checked out the various vendor booths yet, so she took the opportunity. After inspecting a cart next to the entrance to the maze, she turned around and saw Becca.

Becca had her head down and was flipping through a huge stack of pages on an oversized clipboard. By the looks of it, there had to be at least a hundred pieces of paper. She finally looked up, saw Candace, waved, and came over.

"Glad to see you're doing better," Becca said.

"Thanks. What is that?" Candace asked, pointing with a crutch toward the clipboard.

Becca's eyes widened. "Charts, grids, maps, searching zones, employee schedules, statistical models, you know, that kind of thing."

"What on earth for?"

"The golden candy cane. I'm going to find it. Then that gingerbread house will be mine."

She drifted toward the gingerbread house as she spoke. Her hand descended on the post that marked the beginning of the hedge maze and one of the two security guards stationed next to the gingerbread house stepped forward and called out. "That's close enough, Becca. You know the rules."

Becca stuck her tongue out at him before removing her hand and backing ten steps away. Then she raised her fist and shook it. "That gingerbread house will be mine!"

"They won't even let you in the maze?" Candace asked.

Becca shook her head. "That's okay. I searched the entire maze before they caught me with this," Becca said, pulling a little baggie out of her pocket. Inside it was a massive purple gumdrop.

"That's not from the house!"

"Yes, it is."

"Why haven't you eaten it yet?" Candace asked, briefly considering calling one of the security guards over to take it from her.

"I'm saving it for something ... special," Becca said, gazing lovingly at the gumdrop.

Candace shivered. She could only imagine what that would be. "Give me fair warning before, okay?"

Becca nodded. "See ya later. I've got more places to search."

Candace watched her go. Part of her hoped Becca found the golden candy cane. Another part of her, though, was rising to the challenge. Maybe she could find the candy cane. After all, she had as good a chance as anyone, even if she was on crutches.

She glanced at her watch and realized she was out of time. She walked over and saw that she would be replacing Lisa. She tensed, really not in the mood to be sniped at.

"You can go," Candace said as she walked up.

"Thank you," Lisa said, face pale and hair unnaturally stiff in weird places and completely limp in others.

Candace blinked in surprise. "Are you okay?" she asked.

Lisa shook her head. "A kid threw up on me today. Twice."

"Gross!"

"I need to go shower."

"I think there might be something wrong with your hair spray," Candace said, staring at the mess on Lisa's head.

"That's not hair spray. It's Lysol," Lisa said before shoving the candy cane basket at her and staggering off.

Candace actually felt sorry for her. As much as she didn't like Lisa, she wouldn't wish that on anyone.

Candace turned her attention to the candy cane basket in her hands. Suddenly, she was aware of the folly of what she was about to do. How was she going to manage the crutches, the candy canes, and the presents? What had she been thinking? What if a little kid accidentally ran into her or kicked her? Worse, what if there was another brat who attacked her?

"Candace, we got this for you," another elf said, walking up and carrying a tall stool with a backrest. He helped her hop up on it. Once seated, she was able to dangle her injured leg on the side away from Santa. Next the elf leaned a pole with a plastic hook on the end against the rope next to her.

"What's that for?" she asked.

"We put ribbons on the packages, so when you want to give out a present, you just have to hook one with this," he said.

"Wow. Thank you!"

"Thank you," he said, giving her a little salute before dashing off.

She turned to look at the stage and thought, *Let them come!*

The kids came in a steady stream, but each of them kept a respectful distance away from her and reached to take the candy canes from her fingers. She was amazed at how quiet and well behaved they all seemed. Maybe they were less rowdy on weeknights because they didn't have to wait quite so long in line.

When her break came, she was surprised to see Kurt walk up. He helped her down off the stool and then walked with her as she tried to limber up.

"You're doing really well," he said.

"Thanks. I have to convince my doctor to let me out of this thing before Winter Formal," she said.

"Hey, no worries. I'm sure we'll be fine even if you're still wearing it. Maybe we'll invent the Don't Go Near the Injured Leg dance."

"Ha ha," she said, although she truly appreciated what he said.

"Everything going okay?"

"Yeah. I was really nervous when I got here, but I didn't need to be. All the kids have been really good. It's like they're going out of their way to avoid touching me at all."

"That's probably because there's a rumor going round that the elf with the crutches uses them to beat naughty children."

"That's terrible!"

"It keeps them from bumping your leg."

"I've only been back two hours. How on earth could a rumor start that quickly?" she asked.

"Maybe because I started it early last week," Kurt said with a smile.

"You!" she asked, feeling somewhat angry.

"Yow. Looks like I'm at the top of your naughty list."

"Kurt, how could you? It's not true!"

"Hey, I didn't want you to come back and risk getting hurt again," he said, suddenly serious. "I figured anything I could do to keep someone from accidentally bumping you or especially from intentionally hurting you is my duty as a boyfriend."

Lying was wrong. She couldn't fault his logic, though. At any rate, the damage was done, and as much as she didn't like admitting it, his tactic seemed to be working.

"Okay, but if I get any supervisors breathing down my neck, I'm pointing them straight at you," she said.

"Fair enough."

He kissed the tip of her nose. "You really are an adorable elf."

She smiled.

10

Candace had Tuesday and Wednesday afternoons off from work. On Tuesday afternoon she made another trip to the mall to buy presents. This time she didn't have her mom or Tamara with her. Mom had dropped her off. It was just her, the shopping list, and the stores. She wore a backpack to carry her purchases, so she still had her hands free to deal with the crutches.

After much indecision she had decided to buy something cool for Josh and small, fun gifts for Sue, Becca, Roger, Martha, and Pete. As it turned out, small and fun were surprisingly hard to come by without adding the word *expensive*.

Pete turned out to be the easiest. She found a book about trains on the discount rack at Barnes and Noble. She also found a book there about the history of chocolate but figured it would be cruel to give it to Becca. Instead, she opted for a small box of sugar-free confections from See's. She thought about writing *sugar free* in bold across the box with a Sharpie so Gib wouldn't have a heart attack when he saw it, but then decided it would look too tacky.

For Roger she found a keychain-sized electronic basketball game that seemed perfect. For Martha she got a World's Best Boss mug. It was totally cheesy, but she had a feeling it would make Martha smile. For Josh she got a Make Your Own pizza package, which included a pizza pan and tons of recipes. For the number of bets they had made that somehow involved pizza, it seemed appropriate. She figured she'd write an obnoxious note to the effect that he was going to have to make her pizza.

When her thoughts turned to a gift for Sue, she remembered that she still hadn't found out why the other girl was so sad and what she could do to help her out. Truth was, Candace had been pretty busy the last week and a half trying to figure out how to help herself.

She decided to hold off buying Sue's present until she had a chance to talk to her more. That meant that Sue and Kurt were the only ones Candace still had to buy for. She stayed for a while longer, trying to find something for Kurt but finally gave up in defeat and called her mom.

On Wednesday afternoon before Bible study, she headed back to the mall with Tamara. With only a week and a half left before Winter Formal, it was time to get serious about dresses.

"So, how freaked are you about auditions in drama Friday?" Tamara asked.

"Totally," Candace answered. "You know I'd be happy to stay in the background, singing in the chorus or something. I definitely don't want to be front and center."

"You always say that and yet—"

"Hey! I'm serious. No public singing."

"What do you think about this?" Tamara asked, pulling a long purple dress off the rack.

"You always wear purple," Candace pointed out.

"And I always look good."

"True. Still, it's Winter Formal. Try something more . . . wintery."

"Wintery? That's good. Don't let the English teacher catch you saying stuff like that. She'll bite your head off."

"What do you think of this one?" Candace asked, pointing to a rich green velvet dress.

"Girl, you are so the pot calling the kettle black. If I always wear purple, you always wear green."

"Come on, I've got red hair. There are some colors that just don't work for me, and one that definitely does."

"That's it. You're not allowed to pick out your own dress," Tamara said.

"What?"

"Nope, forget it. You'll try on the ones I pick for you and buy one of those."

"Fine. Then you have to do the same," Candace said.

"Fine."

Candace went to work and before long had picked five dresses for Tamara to try. "Here you go, white, red, ice blue, forest green, and fuchsia."

"I'm so not wearing the pink one."

"That's for me to decide, remember?"

"Fine," Tamara said with a sigh. "But you get to try on these," she said thrusting the hangers toward Candace.

"Gold, black, peach, burgundy, and brown. Seriously?"

"Seriously."

"They're all short. I was hoping to wear something longer."

"Cand, you know I love you, so I'm going to be honest with you. There's no way you're getting out of that brace before the formal. A short dress will be easier, and we can color coordinate that brace somehow."

Candace was sick of the brace. It was hot, scratchy, and made movement practically impossible. For a week and a half she had been sleeping on her back all night, unable to roll onto her side. There was no way she wanted to wear it to Winter Formal. However, she wasn't stupid enough to stop wearing it until her doctor gave permission.

"Fine," she grumbled.

Tamara carried all the dresses back to the dressing rooms and set Candace up in a large one with a bench she could sit on. "If you need help, let me know. Otherwise, I'll see you in a minute for the first modeling."

A few minutes later, Candace had struggled into the brown dress. When she saw Tamara in the fuchsia dress, she laughed hysterically at the look on her best friend's face.

"I told you, I'm not wearing this," Tamara growled.

"The color's great on you, but the style … what is that? Baggy chic?"

"I'd have to say the same thing for yours."

"Next!" they shouted together.

Candace was not thrilled with either the peach or the black dresses, and Tamara similarly dismissed her green and blue dresses. They retreated back into their dressing rooms, and Candace tried on the burgundy dress.

"You know, Kurt's going to think you look great no matter what you wear," Tamara said.

"And you will look great no matter what you wear," Candace said. "Have you asked anyone yet?"

"No," Tamara admitted as she walked into the hall wearing the white dress. It looked stunning against her olive skin. Candace was also surprised by how well the burgundy looked on her. She would have never picked it out, but it was nice.

"Now I think we're getting somewhere," Tamara said.

Only one dress left for each. Candace pulled on the gold one and admired herself in the mirror. It looked awesome and fit really well. She hobbled out into the hall and Tamara appeared in the red dress.

"Wow!" they said in unison.

"And I think we have the winners," Tamara said.

"Good choice. I really like this," Candace said, smoothing down the gold skirt.

"Ditto. I don't usually wear red, but apparently I should."

A minute later they were back in their street clothes and Candace handed the gold dress to Tamara to carry.

"So, who are you taking to the dance?"

"I'm thinking of not taking anyone. There's just no one that I'm interested in right now."

Suddenly, a thought occurred to Candace.

"I'm not sure I like that smile," Tamara said. "I already told you I'm not asking Josh."

"Actually, I was just thinking. If you're not interested in anyone, you have the chance to do a good deed."

"Okay, I'll bite. What do you have in mind?"

"Roger is chewing himself up over the fact that Becca's going to the dance."

"Oh, I see. You want me to take Roger in the hope that he'll be man enough to dance with her and sweep her off her feet."

"Something like that."

Tamara sighed. "Fine. As long as he's clear that that's what's going down."

"I can promise he will be."

"Okay. Set it up."

"Thanks, Tam, you're the best."

"I know."

They reached the register, and Tamara handed the clerk both dresses. "It's on me, although for this favor, you should be buying."

"I can buy my own. Paychecks—amazing things," Candace said.

Tamara rolled her eyes. "You figured out what you're getting Kurt yet?"

"You know I haven't."

"Then save your money in case you need to spend it on his present."

From the mall they headed to Bible study. Jen was already there when they arrived. She looked up at Candace, appearing more timid than she usually did. Candace still hadn't entirely figured Jen out. She was so quiet it was almost unnatural at times. Jen walked over and stared down at the floor. Her shoulders were hunched, and her hands were rammed into her pockets.

"Candace, can I talk to you?" the girl asked.

"Sure, what about?"

"It's about my friend. Well, actually me. Well, my friend and me."

"Okay."

"You see, my best friend isn't a Christian. I've talked to her about it loads of times, but ..."

"What is it?"

"I feel like we're drifting apart now that we're in high school. Her idea of fun is going to these parties, and I don't feel comfortable at them."

"Why? Are people drinking?" Candace asked, thinking about Kurt's Halloween party that she had herself left for that very reason.

"And smoking. It just seems dumb. Does that mean that I'm immature or something?"

"No. If anything, it means that she is. She's playing at being a grown-up without understanding what that really means. To be mature and grown-up means to take responsibility for your own actions, not to do whatever you want."

"That's kinda what I thought," Jen said. "I just don't want to lose my friend."

"Are you worried about losing your only friend, or are you worried about losing her specifically?" Candace asked.

"I'm not sure."

"Well, I can tell you this. You can always make new friends. And true friendship can survive just about anything."

"Thanks."

"Does that help at all?"

Jen nodded. Other girls started arriving and she moved away.

"Well said," Tamara said softly.

"I hope so."

Once everyone had arrived, they went around the circle and discussed what they had done to grow in their target area in the past week. Most of the progress was small, but hard won.

"I didn't smoke once this week, even when my mom yelled at me," the one girl said.

"That's awesome," Candace said. Not only could she not imagine smoking, she couldn't imagine having a mom that constantly yelled at her. She thanked God quietly for a good home life.

"I prayed in the morning while I showered instead of at night so I wouldn't fall asleep," Jen said shyly.

"Good for you," Tamara said. "I tried that once, and I still fell asleep."

"What do you do?" Jen asked.

"I pray when I drive," Tamara answered.

Candace looked at her in surprise. They had been friends for thirteen years, and that was a new one. It just went to show that no matter how well you knew someone, they could still surprise you.

When it was Joy's turn, she smiled at everyone. "I managed to up my devotion and prayer time with God to two hours every day."

Candace just stared at her, and all she could think was that either Joy was lying or she had no life whatsoever. What was worse was seeing the look of discouragement on the other girls' faces when they heard that. *All she's doing is making everyone feel that there's something wrong with them. Why does she do that?*

Candace cleared her throat. "Good for you," she said. "It must be awesome to have no work, family, or school commitments in the evening so that you can do that." She tried to keep her tone light.

"Oh, no," Joy said, wide eyed. "I'm very busy. But I think God's worth it, don't you?"

For the first time, Candace actually thought about using her crutch on someone. She gritted her teeth. She didn't know how to move past this without ripping into Joy or completely dousing the other girls' sense of self-worth.

"God is worth everything," Candace said quietly. "But all he asks of each of us is our best. Clearly, some have more time, some have more ability, and some have more humility," she said.

She was walking a fine line, and she knew it. Joy's eyes narrowed as though she suspected she had just been slammed. She wasn't sure, though, and Candace could use that to her advantage.

"I'm very proud of the progress we've all made. It sounds like some major battles have been fought and won in people's lives."

At the end of the study, Candace climbed into Tamara's car and fumed as soon as they pulled out of the church parking lot. "Why does she have to do that? What's with the holier-than-thou thing? I mean, seriously, that doesn't help anyone. It just discourages the girls who are actually trying."

"Maybe she's insecure," Tamara suggested.

"Do you really think that?"

"No, but I'm trying to find a way to keep you from punching her lights out next week."

"I'm so glad you never play those games," Candace said with a sigh.

"No. However, I have been known to play richer-than-thou games with people who make me mad."

"I think I've seen that," Candace said, smiling at the memories.

"Maybe Joy doesn't even realize what she's doing. Who knows, maybe her parents do that, and she thinks it's what's expected."

"So, you think I should try to talk to her."

"At least find some common ground or a way to tolerate her."

As much as she didn't want to admit it, she knew Tamara was right.

❄

On Thursday Candace arrived at The Zone early to hunt down Roger. She asked a ref, who had seen him heading toward the Thrill Zone a few minutes earlier.

She hobbled her way there. It was getting easier to use the crutches now that she was putting her full weight on both legs. Her shoulder felt better too.

When she got into the Thrill Zone, she saw a group of referees huddled around the Spiral roller coaster, staring and pointing upward. Candace stopped and looked up. Becca walked along the tracks, head swinging back and forth.

"What is she doing?" Candace asked.

"Looking for the golden candy cane," someone nearby said.

"She's going to hurt herself!"

"Yeah, but you got to admire her dedication."

"Go, Becca!" someone else shouted.

"But surely it couldn't be up there!" Candace protested.

"Why not?" Roger asked as he walked over, eyes still staring skyward.

"That's absurd."

"Not really. Two dozen referees have already gone over every inch of the off-field areas with no luck. That leaves areas on field that only referees can get to. This certainly counts."

"But no sane person would put it up there!"

"Have you met all the Game Masters? I'm quite sure at least a couple of them are certifiable."

"But she could fall!"

"Not Becca," someone said.

"She's got great balance; she used to be a dancer," someone else pointed out.

Candace couldn't believe how calmly everyone else seemed to be taking Becca's high-wire act.

Finally Roger turned and looked at Candace. She could see that his face was pale, and there was fear in his eyes. "Do you honestly think you could stop her?" he asked.

"No," Candace admitted, "even if I had two good legs."

"Exactly. If you find a way to get her off there now, she'll just be back. She's almost done; it's better to let her finish."

"She certainly is taking this candy cane hunt to new heights," Candace said, wincing at her own pun.

Three minutes later Becca finished. She jumped back down onto the loading deck, and everyone gave her a round of applause. She blushed and did a little curtsey before retrieving her clipboard and heading for the exit.

"She's amazing," Roger said wistfully as he watched her go.

"Roger."

"Yeah?"

"Actually I was looking for you."

"What's up?" he asked.

"I was thinking. I have a way that you could go to the Winter Formal and have a chance to sweep Becca off her feet."

"How?" he asked, eyes wide.

"You could go with my friend, Tamara—strictly platonic of course. She said she'd take you as a favor to me so that you could get a chance to be there with Becca."

"That would be awesome!" he said, grabbing her in a bear hug. "Oh, sorry," he said, pulling away as she winced.

"I'm okay. So, would that be cool?"

"Yes."

"Great."

"What color dress will she be wearing?"

"Becca? I don't know."

"No, Tamara. I should at least get her a corsage as a thank you."

"Oh. Red."

"Cool."

"I'll see you later then," Candace said as she headed back toward the Santa Zone.

As she climbed up on her stool and accepted the basket of candy canes, she couldn't get Roger and Becca out of her mind. Soon her thoughts drifted to Becca's search for the golden candy cane.

"Now, if I were a Game Master, where would I hide that golden candy cane?" Candace asked herself. The obvious answer was in one of the baskets of real candy canes that they used in the "Santa Zone," as she had started calling the area.

That didn't seem quite fair, though, since it would distinctly narrow the field of possible refs who could find it. No, it would either have to be somewhere isolated where no one was likely to find it, or somewhere everybody went on a regular basis. Since it seemed like it definitely wasn't off field, that would severely limit the possibilities for the latter group.

"So, where does nobody go, and where does everybody go?"

Becca would know the answer. Then again, somebody else might have already found the candy cane. She had to believe, though, that it wouldn't be that easy to find. It would take skill, perseverance, and lots and lots of luck. That's how she'd set it up if she were a Game Master.

11

On Friday morning Candace considered staying in bed. She really was not looking forward to auditions in drama class. She knew she'd never hear the end of it from Tamara, though. Reluctantly, she got up.

By the time she made it to drama, she was so nervous she thought she might be sick. Tamara didn't look any better than Candace felt. Mr. Bailey, however, had never looked better. He was laughing and jumping around the stage, his impossibly long legs bending in every direction as though he were a rag doll.

"Okay, class, as you know, today we are auditioning. First, we'll sing a little, and then each of you will read a couple pages of the script."

He sat down at the piano. "Ladies first. Gather around here."

Candace stood up and hobbled over to stand next to Tamara.

First he played a series of notes, asking them to sing "La" to each of them. After that, he had them sing "Row, Row, Row Your Boat." After a few minutes he let them sit down and had the boys come forward and do the same.

"Good!" he said, standing up and taking a seat with the rest of the class. He picked up a clipboard and shuffled some papers.

"Now, I'm going to have you read some scenes. Let's start with Candace and Greg. You don't have to go up on the stage ... just stand in front of it."

Candace grabbed her copy of the scene from Mr. Bailey as she hobbled to the front. Candace felt herself beginning to sweat as she glanced at the lines for Aldonza, the female lead.

"And action!" Mr. Bailey said.

Candace read the lines with as much feeling as she could. Better that than for Mr. Bailey to ask her to do it over. When they reached the end of their scene, he asked them to read for two different characters. Then he asked them both to sit down, and he called up Tamara and one of the other guys.

Incredibly, everyone had auditioned before class came to an end.

"Excellent," Mr. Bailey said, smiling. "You all did a fine job. I'll be posting the cast list before Christmas break."

Candace was relieved. That way she wouldn't have to spend the break worrying about what she was going to have to do. She would already know, and hopefully the news would be good.

"You were awesome!" Tamara said as they headed for their lockers.

"Please," Candace said.

"Truly."

"I thought you did really well."

Tamara shook her head. "I did okay, but I think he's got his eye on you for the lead."

"I have a hard time believing that. Besides, it's not just about acting, it's also about singing, which I've never done before."

"You sounded just as good as anybody else," Tamara pointed out.

"I refuse to stress about it until I have more information," Candace said.

"Candace, you totally rocked!" one of the guys said as he walked by.

Tamara raised an eyebrow. "Is that enough new information?"

Candace just shook her head.

❄

When she got to The Zone, Candace was a couple minutes early but decided to head for her post anyway. She saw that she would again be taking over for Lisa.

"Hey," Candace said as she hobbled up.

"You know, I can't figure you out," Lisa admitted.

Okay, totally random.

"What do you mean?" Candace asked.

"No matter what happens to you, you keep coming back for more."

Candace shrugged. "I don't think it's all that unusual."

"Yes, it is. Even after what I did to you over the summer, you can still be civil to me. What is that?"

Candace took a deep breath. "I don't want to be," she admitted. "I want to hate you, but that's not what God wants. Don't get me wrong, I really don't like you, but ..." She shrugged. It sounded pathetic, even to her. She just wasn't sure how to express it all.

"So, you're what, a Christian?"

"Yes."

"What's that like?"

Candace just stared at her for a minute. She wasn't exactly sure what Lisa was asking, and she was even less sure how to answer her. "Well, it's good. I mean, no matter how bad things get, I know I'm never alone."

"Do you really think God answers prayer?"

Candace thought of the miserable night she had spent trapped in The Zone and the miracle when she had actually won the most impossible game in the midway area. "Absolutely."

"I tried praying once that Kurt and I would get back to-gether," Lisa said.

Candace really wasn't sure how to answer that one. She sighed.

"Why do you like Kurt?" Candace asked, surprising herself.

"I like him because he doesn't care about next week or next month or next year. It makes him easy to be with. He's so different than my father. My dad is all about the bottom line, the end goal, the plan."

Candace was struck by the irony of it. The very thing she couldn't stand about Kurt was the thing that Lisa loved.

"You know," she said slowly. "Sometimes God takes a long time to answer prayer. It's about His timing, not ours. Kurt and I aren't married or anything like that. I mean, who knows what the future will bring." She swallowed and then said one of the hardest things she had ever said in her whole life. "If God wants the two of you to be together, nothing will stand in the way."

Lisa hugged her tight and then let her go again before Candace could even react. "I still hate you," Lisa said.

"Okay."

"Okay."

Lisa walked off, and as Candace watched her go, she asked God, "What was that all about?"

He didn't answer, but she could feel in her heart that the meeting had not been coincidental.

She settled herself on top of the stool and began to distribute the candy canes. She couldn't figure out what was up with Lisa, so she tried to think about something else, like the golden candy cane and where it might be and whether Becca already had it.

For a Friday afternoon, it was a lot slower than she had expected it to be, and she was able to do some people watching. She noticed clusters of referees in regular clothes walking around with heads together and clipboards in hand. *They must be taking a page from Becca's playbook*, Candace thought as she watched them. The closer it got to the Christmas party, the more desperate people were in searching for the golden candy cane.

When she finally got her dinner break, she walked over to the Muffin Mansion, curious to find out how Becca was doing with her search. She walked inside and saw George, one of the referees from the Splash Zone, standing in the middle of the room looking miserable.

"What do you mean you don't get it?" Gib was asking.

"Just what I said, I don't get it."

"How do you not get it?"

"I don't know. Maybe because my parents never told me?"

"That's absurd."

"Well, it's true. Can you help me or not?"

"What don't you get?" Candace asked, unable to remain quiet.

"Christmas."

"What about it?"

"What is it?" he asked.

"What do you mean, what is it?" Candace asked.

"See, there you have it!" Gib said.

Candace couldn't help but feel like she was in some sort of farce. She turned to look at Gib. "I don't get it."

"He doesn't know what Christmas is all about!" another Muffin Mansion referee finally shouted from the back.

"What Christmas is all about?" Gib asked disbelievingly. "I'll tell you what Christmas is all about."

He struck a pose that seemed oddly familiar. He cleared his throat and began. "And it came to pass in those days, that there went out a decree from Caesar Augustus, that all the world should be taxed. And this taxing was first made when Cyrenius was governor of Syria. And all went to be taxed, every one into his own city. And Joseph also went up from Galilee, out of the city of Nazareth, into Judaea, unto the city of David, which is called Bethlehem; because he was of the house and lineage of

David: To be taxed with Mary his espoused wife, being great with child."

"Being what with what?" George interrupted.

"That is, being pregnant," Gib said. "May I continue?"

"Yeah, sure."

Gib cleared his throat again and carried on. "And so it was, that, while they were there, the days were accomplished that she should be delivered. And she brought forth her firstborn son, and wrapped him in swaddling clothes, and laid him in a manger; because there was no room for them in the inn."

"Which inn?"

"Any inn, all inns. Just listen to the story!" Gib bellowed.

"Sorry."

Gib continued. "And there were in the same country shepherds abiding in the field, keeping watch over their flock by night. And, lo, the angel of the Lord came upon them, and the glory of the Lord shone round about them: and they were sore afraid. And the angel said unto them, Fear not: for, behold, I bring you good tidings of great joy, which shall be to all people. For unto you is born this day in the city of David a Saviour, which is Christ the Lord. And this shall be a sign unto you; Ye shall find the babe wrapped in swaddling clothes, lying in a manger. And suddenly there was with the angel a multitude of the heavenly host praising God, and saying, Glory to God in the highest, and on earth peace, good will toward men. And it came to pass, as the angels were gone away from them into heaven, the shepherds said one to another, Let us now go even unto Bethlehem, and see this thing which is come to pass, which the Lord hath made known unto us. And they came with haste, and found Mary, and Joseph, and the babe lying in a manger."

"Luke, chapter two, verses one through sixteen," Candace said softly. The passage never failed to move her, and she could tell from the passion in his voice that it moved Gib as well.

"Okay, I didn't understand it when Linus said it in the 'Charlie Brown Christmas' show, and I really don't get it now," George said.

"What's not to get?" Gib asked, clearly bewildered.

"Let me try," Candace said.

"Aye," Gib conceded.

"Jesus, born to be the Savior of the world, was born in a barn and put to bed in a trough used by the animals. The first people to hear that he was born were shepherds who were poor. They were told by angels and urged to go see the baby."

"Oh, I get it."

"That you understand?" Gib asked before throwing up his hands and walking away.

"Well, yeah."

George turned back to Candace. "I get it."

"Good."

She turned and walked out. She was beginning to get a headache, and she figured the longer she stayed, the worse it would get. She'd have to find out how Becca was doing some other way. She'd also been toying with asking Gib's advice on what to get Kurt for Christmas, but clearly that could wait.

She was only a few feet from the shop when Becca appeared. "Coming for a muffin?" she asked lightly.

"No," Candace said. "I was coming to see how your golden candy cane hunt is going."

"Good, good, I've eliminated many of the viable possibilities, and I'm confident that I'm closing in on it," Becca said, tapping her massive clipboard.

"I wouldn't go in there right now if I were you," Candace said, indicating the store.

"Ton of whiny players?"

"Theological discussion."

Becca raised an eyebrow but didn't ask.

"So, what do you think I should get Kurt for Christmas?" Candace asked.

Becca smiled. "I can't even figure out whether or not to get Roger something for Christmas."

"I know he's getting you something. Does that help?"

"Yes and no. How's your knee?"

"Better. I'm getting a bit used to the brace and crutches. I figure I'll be able to ditch them just about the time I master them."

"Isn't that always the way?" Becca asked.

"Tell me about it."

"Any more kids try to attack you?"

"No, apparently there's a rumor that I smack naughty kids with my crutches."

"Ah yes, I heard that one. Your legend only grows by the season," she said with a smirk.

Candace rolled her eyes. "I'd trade in legend for quiet and simple any day."

"Really? In my experience, quiet and simple are overrated."

"With you, I didn't even realize they were an option," Candace teased.

"You know me," Becca said. "Well, I better get back before they send out a search party. See ya."

Candace continued walking back toward the Holiday Zone. She was no closer to finding Kurt a present than she was in finding the golden candy cane. She just hoped they didn't both prove completely elusive.

12

Come Tuesday afternoon Candace still couldn't figure out what to get Kurt for Christmas. She was starting to get desperate and had even briefly considered asking Lisa's opinion on the subject. She walked around the different vendor booths but didn't see anything that grabbed her. Finally, she hunted up Roger in the Dug Out.

"Hey, Candace, what I can do for you?" he asked.

"Has Kurt ever been in here admiring anything?"

"No. Can't figure out what to get him for Christmas?"

"No. Any suggestions?"

"Sorry. I just don't know the guy well enough."

"He's really into history."

"Then get him a book or a model or something."

"I just don't know. I was hoping for something a little more special or personal."

"Well, good luck. If he comes in, I'll make sure to find out what he likes."

"Thanks, Roger," she said before exiting the store.

She tracked down Sue next.

"The last thing I want to even think about right now is Christmas presents," Sue said, scowling as she cleaned the mirrors in the Holiday Zone women's rooms.

"I'm dying here. I can't figure out what to get him."

"Why don't you ask him what he wants?"

"Because I'm too proud to admit to my boyfriend that I have no idea what he would like for Christmas."

"Then maybe he shouldn't be your boyfriend."

"Ouch," Candace said.

"Sorry. Too harsh?" Sue asked, looking over at her.

"Little bit. Are you okay?"

"I'm fine. I'm just sick of cleaning lipstick off the mirrors. Tell me why some people think it's funny to use the glass as a blotter?"

"Haven't a clue."

"I'm tempted to tape a note here saying I use water from the toilets to clean the mirrors so kiss them at your own peril."

"Okay, remind me never to get on your bad side," Candace said.

Sue stopped. "I'm sorry. I'm really stressed right now. I just finished up finals at school, and I'm still playing catch-up. It's not you."

"Is there anything I can do?" Candace asked.

"I don't think there's anything anyone can do," Sue said with a sigh.

"Well, if you change your mind, let me know," Candace said, edging toward the exit.

"Thanks. And if I think of anything for Kurt, I'll let you know."

"I'd appreciate it," Candace said.

When Candace got home, she walked over to her father.

"Dad, you're a guy."

"Thank you for the affirmation," he said.

"I mean, I need a guy's opinion."

"Well, since you've laid the basic groundwork establishing me as a guy, I believe I am qualified to give a guy's opinion," he said with a smirk.

The last thing she needed was lawyer humor, but she smiled anyway.

"Dad, what do you think I should get Kurt for Christmas?" she asked.

"Does he collect anything?"

"I don't know."

"Does he need anything for school?"

"Not that I know of."

"Get him a wallet."

"Too generic."

"Get him a set of golf balls."

"I don't think he plays golf."

"Okay, get *me* a set of golf balls."

"Dad!"

"I'm sorry, honey. I just don't know enough about him to make any kind of reasonable speculation about what he might like. Wish I could help."

"It's okay."

"You could get Josh a board game, though. There's this new one that sounds pretty cool."

"I already got his present," she said.

"Oh. Then get *me* the board game, will you?"

"Good night, Dad."

She headed upstairs and tried to prep for Bible study. She couldn't get the subject of gifts out of her mind, though.

❄

"Next week will be our last meeting before Christmas, and if everyone is interested, I thought we could do a gift exchange," Candace said, addressing the group.

"I don't know," Joy said. "The commercialization of Christmas has hurt the real meaning of the holiday. I don't think it would be a good idea to celebrate by spending money on tacky gifts."

"You know what, Joy? You don't have to be a part of it, but I happen to like giving gifts at Christmas, and I don't see it as commercialism. I see it as a sacred tradition handed down from the wise men to us. And I wasn't suggesting "tacky" gifts or white elephants. I was going to suggest we try to give a gift that has somehow touched us personally. If you're not comfortable with that, or with me, you can feel free to join a different Bible study."

Candace came to a stop. She'd said it. Out loud. There was no taking it back. *I'm so going to be fired as Bible study leader.*

The other girls in the group had their eyes on the ground.

"Well, I have a hard time believing that everyone here agrees with you," Joy said.

"Actually, I do," Jen said, her voice barely more than a whisper.

"What?" Joy asked, eyes blazing.

"You make us all feel like you're judging us, and you think you're better than us," another girl said.

"Just because we can't spend two hours a day in prayer doesn't mean we don't love God and try to follow him," a third girl continued.

Joy stood up and stalked out.

"Now you've done it," Tamara said.

"I better go after her," Candace said, dragging herself to a standing position and grabbing her crutches.

"Please don't," one of the other girls begged.

"I have to. As bad as she makes us feel, I think I just made her feel that way, and that isn't cool."

As much as she didn't want to, Candace forced herself to walk outside in search of Joy. She didn't have to go far. She found the other girl sitting on the curb, knees pulled up to her chest. Candace wished she could sit down beside her, but she hadn't mastered lowering herself that far down yet.

"I'm sorry. That was uncool of me," Candace said. "I guess I let you push my buttons."

"You suck as a leader."

"Well, if you wanted to be the leader so badly, why didn't you volunteer?" Candace asked.

"I did."

Candace was quiet while she took that in. If Joy had volunteered, then there had to be a reason why Pastor Bobby wanted Candace to lead this group of girls and not Joy.

"I'm sorry. I know what's it's like to feel you've gotten the raw end of the deal."

"I doubt that."

"No, trust me on this one."

Joy was silent for a minute, and then Candace heard something that sounded like a sob.

"Joy, what's wrong?" she asked.

"Sometimes I feel like I don't know how to be a Christian," Joy admitted.

That one really threw Candace for a loop. "What do you mean?"

"I don't know what God wants from me. My parents are always pushing me to trust God, trust God. My mom prays constantly. If I ask my dad a question, he just quotes Scripture at me."

"So, in some ways they've messed you up. I'm sorry. Look, I don't have all the answers, but there's one thing I do know. It doesn't matter what *we* do; what matters is what *Jesus* did. No amount of praying can get us into heaven; only He can. I guess I see faith as more of a relationship than anything else. And like all relationships, sometimes I'm an idiot. I say stupid things, get angry, and screw stuff up. The cool thing about God, though, is He doesn't care. He just waits for me to calm down so he can pick me back up."

"You're saying He forgives you."

"Yeah. And I'd like it if you would forgive me too."

"Only if you forgive me for sniping at you."

"Done. Easiest deal I've made in a long time."

Joy stood up and held out her hand. Candace shifted her crutch, and then they shook. "Now let's go inside and discuss meaningful gifts, shall we?"

Joy nodded.

"And while we're talking about that, what would you get a boyfriend for Christmas?"

"How long you been dating?"

"Kinda hard to tell. About five months."

"Serious or not so serious?"

"I'm not sure."

Joy stopped and looked at her like she was crazy. Finally she shook her head. "Until you can answer that question, I don't think anyone's going to be able to help you, Candace."

❆

The next day her mom went with her to her doctor's appointment. Candace had been praying that he would release her from the brace so she wouldn't have to wear it to Winter Formal. Her hopes were dashed, though, when he told her she'd have to wear it at least another week.

"Winter Formal is tomorrow night!"

"Sorry. You'll just have to do the shuffle instead of the tango," he said with a humorless smile.

As soon as they left the office, Candace called Kurt.

"Brace or no brace?" he asked.

"Brace."

"It's okay. You'll look beautiful no matter what you wear."

"That's sweet," she said.

"It's the truth," he countered. "Don't worry, we'll have fun, and I won't let anyone photograph you below the waist."

"Promise?"

"Promise."

She hung up, and a second later her phone rang again. She thought it was Kurt calling right back, but it turned out to be Tamara.

"Brace," Candace said.

"Bummer."

"Thanks."

"Guess what?"

"What?"

"The cast list is out for *Man of La Mancha*," Tamara said, sounding like she was about to burst.

"Already?"

"Yes!"

"And?"

"I'm playing the housekeeper."

"Good for you, although I don't really see you in that part," Candace said.

"And you're the lead."

"What?" Candace asked.

"You're playing Aldonza!"

There was some static, and then another voice said, "Hi, Candace, this is Lila. Congratulations!"

It took all of Candace's willpower to say, "Thanks!"

She so didn't want to be the lead, but it looked like she was stuck with it. The worst thing she could do was show her disappointment in front of someone who probably would have loved to have been in her position.

Tamara got her phone back. "Well?"

"This is a disaster!" Candace said.

"Actually, I think it's hilarious."

"You would," Candace said, making a face even though Tamara couldn't see her.

"Don't forget, I'm going to be on stage too, and not just in the chorus."

"I know," Candace sighed.

"And we're going to have months to practice, so by the time we do perform the play, we could do it in our sleep."

"I hope you're right."

123

"Of course I'm right," Tamara said. "You'll see. Talk to you later."

Candace hung up the phone and closed her eyes.

Her mom coughed. "So, you're going to be the lead?"

"You could hear that, huh?"

"Tamara's loud when she's excited."

"I can't worry about it right now. I just have to stay focused and make it to the New Year."

"Sounds sensible."

"Mom, what do you think I should get Kurt for Christmas?" she asked.

"Something recycled?" she suggested with a smile.

"Somehow I don't think so," Candace said with a wry grin.

"How about a gift certificate?"

"Good, but I was hoping for something more personal."

"Tie?"

"He doesn't really wear them."

"Is there an author he likes or a movie you could get him?"

"I don't know."

"He likes history, right?"

"Yeah."

"Then get him a piece of history."

"Mom, you're a genius!"

That night on Ebay, after hours of searching, Candace found just the right thing. It was a letter written by Benjamin Franklin. Moments before she bid on it, though, she discovered in the fine print that it was a reproduction and not an actual original. When she finally did find an original, the two-thousand-dollar opening bid was enough to make her heart stop.

She thought about continuing on and trying to find something else, but was too discouraged by that point. She was also tired, and she wanted to make sure she got enough sleep before the formal. Frustrated, she crawled into bed and fortunately fell right to sleep.

13

The day of the Winter Formal arrived, and Candace could barely keep still she was so excited. It had been agreed that Kurt and Roger would pick Candace and Tamara up at Candace's house. As soon as school was out, Candace and Tamara headed straight there to get ready.

"What did you have to do to get tonight off?" Tamara asked as they started on their hair.

"I had to trade my shift tonight for one tomorrow night."

"Don't you work tomorrow morning?"

"Yeah, it's not going to be pretty," Candace said.

"I'm thinking not."

After applying all their makeup, they were finally ready for the dresses and the jewelry. Tamara finished her look off with a pair of red heels, while Candace had to be content with gold flats.

Candace sighed as she stared at the brace on her leg. "You know, if I ever find those little brats, they're going to have some explaining to do."

"Hey, at least your leg's not broken," Tamara said.

"I know, but it feels like it is."

"Come on, cheer up. You've done really well with that thing, and I know it's been awful. Kurt doesn't care that you're wearing it tonight, and if you let it bug you, then those bratty kids and their horrible father won," Tamara said.

"You're right. And there's no way I'm going to let that happen," Candace said. "All the bruises have finally gone, and my shoulder's not sore anymore. All in all, I think I'm doing quite well."

"You'd have my vote for Christmas queen."

"If only they crowned a queen and king at the formal," Candace teased.

"I said I'd vote for you; I didn't say I'd actually let you beat me," Tamara said.

"Sorry, that's right. You are the Christmas queen."

The doorbell rang downstairs.

"Now, you're sure Roger's clear on the whole not-really-a-date thing, right?"

"Crystal."

"Good."

They made their way downstairs, and Candace was gratified not only to see that Roger and Kurt looked great, but also they clearly thought she and Tamara looked great.

Both guys presented their offerings of wrist corsages. Then Candace and Tamara pinned boutonnières on them. Candace's dad took the obligatory photos, and they were off.

As if trying to prove that he knew it wasn't a real date, Roger started to take the front passenger seat. Kurt cleared his throat, though, and instead, Roger held the door open for Candace. Then, as though afraid of showing favoritism, he quickly opened the rear door for Tamara.

Candace saw Tamara roll her eyes, and she stifled a giggle. At least when they arrived at the dance, Tamara had the good grace to accept Roger's arm as they walked inside.

Candace smiled as she took in the decorations. Fake snow was piled against the walls, and pale blue lights gave the place a winter wonderland sort of feel. She and Kurt got their picture taken and then found a table at the edge of the dance floor. Roger and Tamara joined them a minute later.

Candace looked around at all the faces, some familiar and some definitely not. Suddenly, her eyes picked out the face she was looking for. "You guys will not believe this," she said.

"What?" Tamara asked.

"Check out Becca," Candace said, pointing toward the dance floor.

Becca was a vision of elegance. She was wearing a pale blue dress with white marabou feather trim. Her hair was swept upward and held in place by a pearl comb. She wore long white gloves and had the most serene smile on her face that Candace had ever seen.

"Wow, she's amazing!" Roger breathed.

"And she's not trying to make a break for the punch bowl," Kurt noted.

"That girl has serious style," Tamara said. She turned and looked at Roger. "You are totally beneath her."

Candace was shocked to hear Tamara say it.

"I know," Roger whimpered.

"But her date is beneath you," Tamara said. "So, go out there and take her away from him."

Roger stood up and moved onto the dance floor. Candace strained but couldn't hear what was being said. A moment later, though, he cut in, and Becca was dancing with Roger.

"They are cute together," Tamara said. "Somebody owes me a dance for this, though."

"I think that can be arranged," Kurt said. "First, though, I'm going to dance with the prettiest girl here."

Candace blushed as he offered her his hand. She walked slowly, carefully onto the dance floor with him. Then she put her arms around his neck. She tried shuffling her feet, but it didn't work out very well. So they just stood and swayed to the music. Candace couldn't stop smiling. It was the first time she had danced with a guy other than her father. She was wearing a brace, hated the song that was playing, and couldn't move across the floor. Yet somehow it was better than she had imagined it could be.

When the music stopped, Kurt walked her slowly back to her chair before dancing one dance with Tamara. Roger came back in the middle of the song, looking sad.

"She's dancing with him again," he said.

"Well, technically, he did bring her," Candace said. "You could dance with Tamara."

He brightened at that. When Tamara and Kurt returned, all four of them went back onto the dance floor.

As the evening progressed, everyone began to relax. Roger and Becca danced several times, and both Candace and Tamara danced at least once with every guy from their drama class.

At one point Candace found herself sitting with both Becca and Tamara. "Having fun?" she asked Becca.

"Quite," Becca said with a gentle smile.

"You look great. So … poised."

"Thank you. It's good to be able to dress up once in a while. It's nice to be around people who don't know me for the most part."

"You mean it's good that nobody's guarding the punch bowl?" Tamara asked with a grin.

Becca nodded. "I can control myself, you know. It just takes a lot of effort, and most days the effort's not worth it. Sometimes too, it's just easier to be what people expect you to be."

Candace looked at her. In many ways Becca had the same problem as Joy and the girls in her Bible study. Maybe everyone had the same problem. There were always other people's expectations to either live up to or downplay. People so rarely got the chance to just be themselves. At The Zone, people expected Becca to be a sugar maniac, and she was. But that wasn't all she was. Sugar mania was just one part of her personality.

Clearly, she also had a more sophisticated side, which she was showing at the moment.

"I told you, too much deep thinking hurts your brain and gives you wrinkles," Tamara teased.

Candace smiled. "You're right. Less thinking, more dancing!"

She danced twice more with Kurt and once with Becca's date. Candace didn't know what it was, but she really didn't like the guy. She was glad when Kurt cut in.

Finally Candace was exhausted. She didn't know how late it was, but she knew she was going to be hurting in the morning when she had to get up.

"Ready to call it a night?" Tamara asked her.

Candace nodded, and Kurt was on his feet in a minute. He walked over and talked to Roger and then came back. "We should have brought separate cars. Roger's going to stay awhile longer. I told him to call if he needed me to come get him. And he's got cab money just in case."

It had been a wonderful evening, brace and all. When they got to Candace's house, Tamara said good night and drove off in her car. Kurt walked Candace to her door and gave her a kiss.

"Thanks for a great night," she said.

"Thank you. I had a nice time."

After Kurt left, Candace made it upstairs and changed in record time. She thought about sending Josh a quick email but was far too tired. She climbed into bed and found herself praying for Roger and Becca.

❄

Candace woke up, her head throbbing from exhaustion. She felt stiff all over. As she lay there, she began to think that she must have been completely insane when she agreed to swap her Friday night shift for a second Saturday shift. Eight a.m. to four p.m. was looking unbearable. Eight a.m. to midnight seemed impossible.

She dragged herself out of bed and somehow got dressed and downstairs. Her mom was already there sipping coffee. "You look dead," she said.

"I feel dead," Candace answered.

"Maybe you should call in sick."

"Can't. I did this to myself on purpose. I have nobody else to blame."

Her mom shrugged her shoulders. "What doesn't kill you —"

"Makes you stronger. I know," Candace said. "But we've already established that I'm dead."

"No, you just look that way."

Candace fell asleep in the car, and she woke with a start when they were parking.

"I hate getting up early on Saturday," her mom admitted.

Candace stumbled twice on her way to the Santa Zone but was able to catch herself both times. She yawned as she picked up her basket and took her seat.

"Morning." An elf named Juliette walked by looking even more tired than Candace.

"You too," Candace said, yawning again.

When the rush of kids arrived, she started to wake up. She was still sore, but at least she was more alert. As she handed out candy cane after candy cane, she thought from time to time about the golden one hidden somewhere in the park.

As her lunch break drew near, Candace couldn't stop thinking about the golden candy cane. She felt sure it had to be somewhere either everyone went or nobody went. Becca had pretty well scoped the entire place out; Candace had seen her a dozen places that nobody went. Maybe that wasn't the key. Maybe the candy cane truly was someplace everybody went.

At noon an elf named Teresa came to give Candace her break. She slid off the stool and walked slowly toward the Cantina. *Where does everyone go?* she kept asking herself over and over. Halfway to the Cantina she stopped.

Everyone goes through the turnstiles at the employees-only entrance. And that entrance puts them inside the park.

Candace turned and started walking to the employee entrance, crutches moving a little more swiftly than usual. When she reached the entrance, she stood for a moment contemplating it. Where on earth could someone hide a candy cane so that everyone wouldn't see it? On a hunch she moved forward and inspected the turnstiles themselves. The rotating bars were just wide enough that they could hide a candy cane. She tugged on the end of one of them but there was no give.

Convinced that she was on to something, though, she went down the row, trying to pull off the end caps of each bar. On the middle turnstile the cap on the third bar she checked had some give. She pulled harder and it came off in her hand. Her heart started pounding and she reached inside with her fingers. They closed around something and she pulled out a rolled up piece of paper. She unrolled it and discovered that somebody had hastily drawn a picture of a candy cane. Beneath it were the words: I already got it. The "i" in it had a little heart drawn over it.

Candace felt her shoulders slump. She had guessed correctly, but she had been too late. She rolled the paper back up and shoved it back inside. At least she knew she could quit looking. Of course now she was dying to know just who had the golden candy cane.

She turned and made her way back to the Cantina, passing several groups of searchers as she did. She drew close to Pete and two other guys who were obviously on the hunt.

"But there's only a few days left to find the golden candy cane!"

"Think. Where haven't we searched?"

"I don't know ... maybe the Jurassic Park ride!"

Pete grabbed the guy by his shoulders and shook him hard. "Pull yourself together, man, that's at Universal Studios!"

Candace bit her lip to keep from laughing. She thought about telling them that it was all over, that someone had found the candy cane, but decided against it. Whoever had found it hadn't made a big public deal about it, obviously wanting people to continue the search. Who was she to deny them the satisfaction?

The afternoon dragged by slowly, and she watched in envy as four o'clock rolled around and Juliette left to go home.

The line of kids was starting to get shorter, which hopefully meant less crankiness. Several children earlier in the day had looked at Candace's pile of presents in a way she hadn't liked. She had to shake a crutch at one of them before he moved on.

At six, someone came to give her a fifteen-minute break. If possible, Candace felt even stiffer than she had when she'd awakened. She ended up just walking slowly around the Holiday Zone for a few minutes, trying to work out the knots in her muscles.

Candace made it back from break just in time to see three familiar faces approach the front of the line. Sue was there with her younger siblings, Gus and Mary.

Candace straightened up as Gus sat down on Santa's lap. "And what can I get for you young man?" Santa asked.

"Santa, can you bring our parents back? They died in May."

Candace blinked hard, shocked to hear what the little boy had said.

Santa's voice was full of sadness when he spoke. "I wish I could, son, but I don't have the power to do that. I know, though, that they're in heaven looking down on you and Mary and loving you both. Someday you'll see them again."

He hugged the little boy before he climbed down off his lap, and Mary climbed up.

"Santa, we don't have a tree or anything, but my sister says we could each ask you for one thing this year. I'd like a new dolly, and Gus would like a basketball."

"I'll do what I can," Santa promised.

Mary climbed down from his lap and headed toward Candace with Gus beside her.

"Merry Christmas, Mary and Gus," Candace said.

"Candy Corn!" Mary said, pleased to see her.

"Not today. Today I'm Candy Cane," Candace said, forcing a smile. She used the hook to fish a present for each child out of the pile.

"You sure have a lot of names," Gus said solemnly.

"You know, I really do," Candace agreed. She handed each child a present, and their eyes grew round with excitement.

Mary hugged hers to her. "Thank you, Candy Cane!"

"You're welcome," Candace said, fighting back tears. She wanted to look at Sue but she couldn't. Everything made sense now. Why Sue needed to go to college close to home, why she needed it to be as cheap as possible, why she had latched on to Candace's mom.

"Why don't you two go down to the nice elf over there and look at your pictures?" Sue suggested.

Gus and Mary scampered off to do as they were told.

"I'm sorry. I wish you hadn't heard that," Sue said softly.

"What happened to them?" Candace asked.

"Car accident," Sue said, her voice strained. "It's just the three of us now."

Candace reached out and hugged Sue. After a moment she broke away. "You're getting a backup of people who need candy canes," she said, sniffing.

"I'm so sorry, Sue," Candace said.

"Thanks," Sue said.

By the time Sue turned and walked away, both of them were crying. Now she knew what was wrong with Sue. She just needed to figure out how she could help.

14

A little before eight p.m., Martha came up. "We're shutting down this side for the night. There aren't that many kids left in the park who haven't seen Santa."

For a moment Candace thought Martha was going to send her home. She was disappointed when Martha continued. "I'm going to move your stool to the other side."

"Oh, okay," Candace said, half falling off.

"You okay?" Martha asked, eyeing her dubiously.

"Winter Formal last night. Double shift today," Candace said.

"This is exactly why we discourage the double shift," Martha said.

"It was the only one I could trade for," Candace said with a yawn.

Over the next hour, the trickle of children practically ceased. There was one ten-minute stretch where no one showed up. She gave serious thought to asking Santa's advice about Kurt, but she restrained herself. Finally at ten Martha came back.

"Okay, we're shutting down for the night," she announced.

Candace got up and put away her things. Santa stood slowly from his chair and then walked toward her. He smiled and then paused next to her. He put a hand on her shoulder and looked at her with his kindly eyes.

"Candace, get him a watch for Christmas." He winked and then continued walking.

"Thank you, Santa!" she called after him.

❄

Candace was only slightly more rested the next morning. Still, she drove to The Zone early, hoping she could find Josh before the park opened. She found him coming out of the Locker Room.

"Josh, can I talk to you for a sec?"

"Sure, what's up?" he asked.

"I think I know of a job for the cheermeister."

He grinned. "I'm all ears."

"I'm trying to figure out how to do a surprise Christmas party for Sue at her house."

"I'm not sure I follow."

"I found out that her parents died in May and she's been raising her little brother and sister by herself. The little girl told Santa that they don't have a tree or anything."

"That's terrible," Josh said, his eyes clouding.

"I know. I thought maybe we could make Christmas for them."

"So, you're thinking turkey, tree, presents, the works?"

She nodded.

"I'm with you. It sounds like a plan. Who else do you want to bring in on this?"

"Well, Roger and Pete for sure."

"Scavenger Hunt team members have to stick together, huh?"

She nodded. "I was also thinking of talking to Becca, Martha, and Kurt."

"It sounds like you know exactly what you want to do. So, what are you needing help with exactly?"

"The planning. Life is crazy at the moment, and I can't even wrap my head around what day we should try to do this, let alone how."

Josh put a hand on her arm. "It's okay, Candace, we'll make this happen. Let me talk to some of the others and see if I can get some details nailed down for you."

"That would be awesome."

❄

As soon as she got off work, Candace got one of the other elves to drop her at the mall. She had to find a watch for Kurt and something for the Bible study gift exchange. In the first store she tried, she found a watch she liked almost immediately. It was silver in color with a chronograph and a flexible metal band. She didn't know why, but it appealed to her, and, at under twenty-five dollars, it appealed to her pocketbook too. She walked out of the store with a vast feeling of relief and headed immediately for Dearborne's Christian Bookstore where she picked up a copy of one of her favorite CDs by Casting Crowns.

Next she headed for the toy store, which was a complete zoo. She hesitated, not wanting to risk injuring her leg in the fray. Finally, she took a deep breath and plunged in. She emerged almost an hour later, but with exactly what she had been looking for. Then she headed home to wrap her finds.

When she got home, she found her mom on the floor in the living room with wrapping paper everywhere.

"Is it safe?" Candace asked.

"Yes, all your presents are wrapped already. Come join me."

"Cool. I need to get some stuff out of my room."

"I'll help."

A few minutes later they were both sitting on the floor wrapping presents. Candace showed her mom the watch she had gotten Kurt. "Nice choice," her mom said.

"Oh, dad wants this new board game."

"I know, it's already under the tree," her mom said.

"And golf balls?"

"Those too."

"So, does he tell you what he wants?"

"He never said a word. I can tell, though."

"You think I'll ever be able to tell like that with Kurt?"

"You'll be able to tell with someone, but whether or not it's Kurt I don't know."

"Don't look," Candace said.

Her mom closed her eyes while Candace slid her present out of a bag and quickly wrapped it.

"Safe."

Her mom opened her eyes and continued with her wrapping.

"I found out last night that Sue's parents died in May in a car crash."

"That's terrible," her mom said, putting down the scotch tape. "I knew there was something wrong there."

"You were right. Josh is going to help me bring Christmas to them one of these nights."

"That sounds nice. If you need help, let me know."

"Thanks. It got me thinking how lost I would be without you and Dad."

Her mom gave her a quick hug. "We're not going anywhere."

Her dad walked into the room. "Presents?"

"No!" Candace and her mom shouted at the same time.

"But I just want to hold one."

"No holding, touching, feeling, sniffing, or hard staring," her mom said.

Candace laughed. She had never once seen a present her father couldn't guess just from holding it. For years they had tried every fake out they could, including wrapping small presents in giant boxes. Nothing worked. The man was unreal.

Candace handed him the package she had already wrapped for Kurt. "Here's what I got Kurt," she said.

He held it for a moment, lifted it up and down, then handed it back. "A watch is a good choice," he said.

Absolutely unreal.

"Now hand me one of mine."

"No!" they chorused again.

"Fine. But I see one of mine under the tree."

"Don't you dare!" her mom threatened.

"Too late, I see it. We'll have a game night. Candace you should invite Josh; he's good at games and seems to like them too."

She thought her mom was going to choke her dad. Dad just craned his neck as he looked toward the Christmas tree. "Aha! Does Josh also play golf?"

Candace picked up a pillow from the couch and threw it at him. "Hey, watch it! Oh wait, I see one of your presents, Candace. I bet it's a—"

Candace stuck her fingers in her ears and her tongue out at him. He left the room grinning.

❄

Candace woke up Monday morning totally grateful for Mr. Bailey. Thanks to drama class, she had no other school for the day. *Field* and *trip* were two of the cheeriest school-oriented words in existence. She put on a pair of baggy pants and a Christmas sweater and then refastened her leg brace over the pants. It was uncomfortable, and it chafed slightly, but it beat the alternative of wearing either shorts or a skirt on the bus.

Tamara picked her up, and they met the rest of the drama class in the school parking lot. They got onto the bus, and Tamara found them seats at the back where Candace could stretch her leg out in the aisle.

"I love *A Christmas Carol*," Candace said.

"I know," Tamara said with a smile. "Every Christmas you talk about it."

"I can't help it; it's such a cool story."

"Oh. You think it's cool that they portray all rich people as bullying their fellow men and bringing misery down on all those around them? It's cool that the only time people accept Scrooge is when he starts giving away his money, whereas they would be scandalized if he asked them to do the same thing? It's cool that the sickness of a little boy is exploited shamelessly, and yet we have no proof that he will actually survive?"

Candace stared at Tamara in surprise. She never would have dreamed that her friend had problems with the story.

Tamara stared at her for a long minute before cracking a smile. "Yeah, I like the story too."

Candace was relieved. "You scared me. How on earth did you even think of all that?"

Tamara shrugged. "My aunt."

"The evil one?"

"Yeah, the one who sold her soul when she was like two."

Candace shivered. "She always creeps me out."

"She creeps everyone out. Mom's threatening to not let her in the house on Christmas this year."

"Seriously?"

"I think she related it to some sort of sacrilege to invite the devil to eat at the celebration of the birth of the Messiah."

Like her daughter, Tamara's mom could occasionally be a bit theatrical. Candace smiled.

They had been riding on the bus for several minutes before Mr. Bailey stood up. "Okay, class, I just want to go over some ground rules. Remember, be polite and be quiet. Respect the other theater patrons. When we go backstage after the show, stick together. Nobody goes wondering off. Otherwise your ghost can participate in the next performance."

Candace laughed and then quickly stopped when she realized she was the only one. She glanced around at some of her bewildered-looking classmates. "I don't think they got the joke," she whispered to Tamara.

"Either that or they just didn't think it was funny."

When they arrived at the theater, Candace and Tamara waited to get off the bus last. Candace hobbled back down the aisle and made it to the curb. A sudden thought occurred to Candace, and she approached Mr. Bailey.

"How am I going to do this with my leg like this?" she asked.

"Don't worry. I got you an aisle seat on the left so you should have plenty of leg room."

"Thank you. I didn't even think about that until now."

"Not a problem. It's a good object lesson, though. There are people who do have to think about that kind of thing every day. Part of being a good actor is learning to understand the challenges that characters face, both emotionally and physically."

Tamara and Candace walked into the theater lobby with Mr. Bailey. "It will be a good thing for you to remember while you are struggling to understand Aldonza. She is nothing like you, yet I think it will serve you well to try to understand the likes of her."

"Really, why?"

Mr. Bailey stopped and looked at her. "Every year I see thirty new students. Every once in a while I discover one who has the makings of a real actor, and once I even discovered one who had the makings of a star. I cherish the ability to teach those students, and they challenge me to grow as an actor as well."

"You don't think I'm one of those, do you?" she asked, surprised.

"No."

That surprised her even more.

He smiled at her obvious confusion.

"What I do see is a young woman with great creative talent and charisma who hasn't yet realized either of those. You'll do special things in this life, Candace, but only if you wake up and truly discover who you are and step out of the comfort zone you've created for yourself. That's why I cast you as the female lead—as Aldonza. You need to be challenged; you need to be pushed. Your life and Aldonza's have nothing in common. You are not a poor prostitute living centuries ago. You're a modern young woman from a nice family who will never know that kind of poverty and degradation. Yet, Aldonza has an image of herself that is totally inconsistent with the image the hero has of her. In the end, she allows his image to transform her and raise her above the life she has chosen. This makes her strive for greatness. In that respect I believe that you and Aldonza have everything in common. Now, let's join the rest of the class and take our seats."

"But, what about Tamara?" Candace burst out.

"Don't drag me into this," Tamara warned.

Mr. Bailey smiled. "Tamara knows exactly who she is, and she draws great friendship and comfort from you. You, on the other hand, try to hide in her shadow."

He turned and walked down the aisle, while Candace stood, shaken to her core.

"I do try to hide in your shadow," she finally said, looking at Tamara.

"I know. I got so used to it that when you started stepping out a bit over the summer I freaked. As soon as I figured out how cool it was and how much closer it made us, I relaxed."

The theater lights flashed. "Time to find those seats," Tamara said, leading the way down the aisle.

The actors were great, and the costumes were perfect, but all Candace could think about was what Mr. Bailey and Tamara had said. So many things that had happened in the past six months seemed to make a lot more sense. When things seemed to go really crazy in her life, then and only then did she step up, take responsibility, and risk something. For some reason she only did that when pushed. At The Zone, every time she tried to blend into the background, God found a way to bring her back front and center.

Now Mr. Bailey had given her the lead role, not because he thought she was a good actress, but because he thought she needed to learn something. She felt grateful for him and grateful for Tamara's support and insight. She wondered what her other friends would have to say about her in this area.

When the play was over, she clapped with everybody else. Once the theater had started to empty, Mr. Bailey gathered everyone together and they walked down toward the side of the stage where they met a crew member.

He opened a door, and they followed him through corridors underneath the stage until they arrived backstage in the dressing rooms. There was one set of stairs that was tricky, but two of the guys from her class picked her up and carried her up before she could even think to ask for help.

They set her down, and Tamara whispered in her ear, "So that's what a girl has to do to get attention around here."

Mr. Bailey introduced them to several members of the cast whom he seemed to know personally. Candace was excited—and then a little embarrassed for not recognizing her earlier—when she realized that Regina was in the play. Regina, or Reggie as Candace knew her, had been one of the maze monsters she had worked with during Halloween. She hadn't read the program so she had no idea what role Regina had played.

Candace gave her a quick hug. "Awesome job!"

"Thanks, I'm so glad you were able to come see it!"

Mr. Bailey laughed. "You'll have to come see Candace play Aldonza this spring."

"Count on it," Regina said with a smile. "And if you ever want to come see something I'm in, let me know," she told Candace.

"Thanks."

They got a tour of the theater and had a chance to meet lots of people and ask a ton of questions. Finally it was time to leave, and they all trooped back to the bus.

Once they reclaimed their seats, Tamara asked, "So, I saw you staring at the stage but you looked lost in thought. How much of that play did you actually see?"

"I'm thinking pretty much zero. I was distracted."

"Pity. It was really good. Of course, it did suffer in one area."

"What's that?"

"It needed a Christmas queen," Tamara said.

Candace laughed. "You're not letting that go, are you?"

"Not even a little bit."

"Fine, then I declare you the Christmas queen."

"It doesn't work that way."

"Then how does it work?"

"Some kind of authority figure has to proclaim me the Christmas queen."

"And I'm not an authority figure?"

Tamara snorted. "Please, you're my best friend. Even if you were an authority figure, it wouldn't be the same."

"Don't say I didn't try."

❄

When Candace got home she IMd Josh.

> *U there?*
> **No.** ☺
> *How's Operation Christmas Carol?*
> **Cool name.**
> *Thanx.*
> **Talked to everybody, and it's a go.**
> *When?*
> **Checked the schedule. Sat looks good.**
> *Evening?*
> **Yeah.**
> *U R Gr8!*
> **Right back at you. Do u know what U R getting Kurt?**
> *Got it! Santa helped.*

Cool deal. I should have asked him about your present.
What did U get me?
Not telling!
Gift exchange Sat?
U bet!
I can't wait for Christmas!
I can't wait for my brother to get home.
What's he like?
Me but bigger.
Seriously?
Yeah. And more ambitious.
What's he going to do now?
Family business.
Kidding?
No.
Cool.
I hope.
Gotta go.
See ya.

Candace was happy for Josh that his brother was coming home. She couldn't imagine how much he must have missed him. She also couldn't imagine how terrified she would be if she had a brother who was serving in Iraq.

15

On Tuesday afternoon Becca approached her at work. The lines were short, the sun was hot, and Candace was glad for the distraction. Becca stood, eyes bright, but arms folded nonchalantly as she rocked back and forth on her heels. For a moment Candace thought for sure she was going to start whistling.

"So," Becca said, "what's this I hear about Operation Christmas Carol?"

Candace smiled. She had been inspired to use that name after going to see the play. She also laughed because she finally figured out what Becca was doing. She was trying to do the whole clandestine secret-agent-meeting thing.

Candace played along. She turned so she wasn't looking directly at Becca when she spoke. "Last Saturday at 1815 hours, an agent discovered that Christmas was likely skipping a certain house where a referee and her two siblings live. As soon as the information came to my attention, I contacted one of our men in the field, a cheermeister. An operation to rescue this house from its sad holiday vacuum is set to be executed this Saturday at 1800 hours."

"What's my role?"

"Your mission, should you choose to accept it, is to bring food, gifts, and Christmas cheer and to help make such a celebration as will live on in the memories of all who attend."

"Downside?"

"None," Candace answered.

"Sweet. I'm totally there."

"Shall we synchronize our watches?"

"No, just make sure you're on Zone Standard Time."

Candace couldn't keep it up any longer. "Zone Standard Time? What on earth is that?"

"The official time at The Zone as measured by the time clock in the Locker Room," Becca said.

"Ah. So how did things end up at the dance after we left?" Candace asked.

Becca rolled her eyes. "My date turned out to be grabby."

"Eew. Did Roger rescue you?"

"He did."

"And?" Candace prompted, hoping for a fairy tale ending.

"He didn't know what to do next."

"So, how was it left?"

"Same old, same old."

Candace sighed. "Sometimes I think I'm going to have to hit him over the head with a two-by-four."

"You and me both. Well, I gotta get back."

"See ya."

Half an hour later Pete showed up, startling Candace. "So, Saturday night we're helping out Sue and the kids?" he asked without preamble.

"Yes."

"Good. Me and the boys will bring the tree and the trimmings. I just hate the thought of those kids not having Christmas. Everyone should have Christmas."

"Thanks for helping, Pete."

"Thanks for asking. You know, most folks around here make their friends and that's it. Not you. You're always reaching out."

"It doesn't seem that way to me," she said. "I don't know even a quarter of the names of the regular referees."

He smiled. "Every one of them knows yours, though. What I mean is, you bring good things to this place," he said. "People respect you for that. You're friendly to everybody no matter what, and I appreciate that. Most of the year I hate most people. Christmas is the one time of year that it's different. I think it's because overall people are happier or at least are trying to be."

"Thanks, Pete," she said.

"Ain't nothing. Just thought you should know."

Then he turned and walked off, leaving her to marvel over what he had said.

Over the course of the next hour, Martha, Kurt, and Roger also dropped by. Candace seemed to be the information clearinghouse, and she was glad she could answer their questions. When Sue walked up, though, she nearly jumped out of her skin.

Who told her? she thought.

"Candace, I wanted to apologize again for the other day when I was so cranky."

"No worries," Candace said, forcing a smile.

"I was thinking about it. I think the important thing when you give someone a gift is to give it from the heart. I know that sounds a lot like "it's the thought that counts," but it's more than that. A gift is almost like your wish for that person. It's like your wish for them to be entertained or healthy or informed or inspired. So, whatever you get Kurt, just make sure it comes from the heart."

"Thanks, that's a beautiful thought," Candace said.

Sue shrugged. "It's just a question of what you want for that person."

"I want Kurt to be happy," Candace said.

"Really? Is that all?"

"No," Candace admitted. "I want him to be happy, and I want him to be right for me."

"If you're meant to be together, he will be," Sue said.

"Thanks."

"Well, I'm off, and I have to get home."

I wish for you to have joy and hope again, Candace thought as she watched her friend go.

❋

The next night Candace and Tamara showed up at Bible study early so they could set everything up. They had with them an assortment of cookies and the punch Candace's mother was famous for. They set the food up on a couple of card tables and then put their presents on another one.

"Are we going to do the thing where we draw numbers and then go in order and either choose a gift from the table or steal one from someone else?" Tamara asked.

"That's what I was thinking, unless you have a better idea."

"This is your shindig, not mine," Tamara said.

They finished setting up as everyone arrived.

Soon everyone had punch and a stack of cookies as they claimed their seats in the circle.

"Candace, can I talk to you for a minute?" Joy asked.

"Sure," Candace said, retrieving her crutches and walking with Joy out of earshot of the others. She could feel herself tensing up, wondering what the other girl wanted.

"A thought came to me as I was driving over here tonight that it would be cool if each of us gave our present to a person we felt could use it," Joy said. "We don't have to. I mean, whatever you want to do is fine."

"I think that's a great idea," Candace said. "Let's do that."

"Don't tell everybody it was my idea."

"I will tell everybody. When you have something special to contribute, people should know."

Candace made it back to her chair. "Okay, Joy had the coolest idea. We're going to try something. We're going to draw numbers to see who gets to go first. Then, instead of picking presents, we're going to give our present to the person we think could use it most. Now, it will only work if everybody gets a gift. Hopefully, there aren't twelve presents there that will only appeal to three people."

"Good idea, Joy," one of the other girls was quick to say.

They all drew numbers. Candace had number twelve.

"Okay, who has number one?" Candace asked.

"I do," Joy said. She picked a large, thin package off the table and handed it to Candace.

For just a moment Candace wondered if it was all a trick to get her to open this particular box. Maybe Joy had found a way to get back at her. She took a deep breath, and forcing a smile, opened the package.

It was a painting of a ballerina alone in the center of the stage, poised to begin dancing. A solitary beam of light was before her, but only her toe was in it, as though she wasn't quite ready to step completely into it. It was one of the most haunting images Candace had ever seen.

"It's beautiful!" Candace said.

"I painted it six years ago."

"You did this?" Candace asked, amazed.

Joy nodded. "When I created it, I called it Fear. I've renamed it, though. It's called Faith."

Candace wanted to say thank you, but the words caught in her throat. She could feel the tears welling up behind her eyes.

"So, share already!" Tamara said, breaking the spell and forcing Candace to smile instead.

She turned it around so that everyone could see it. She could tell that they were all as impressed as she had been with Joy's skill. She could also tell that none of them saw exactly what she saw.

"Okay, number two. Who has number two?" Candace asked.

One of the junior girls went, followed by two of the sophomores. Tamara had number five, and she handed the small package to Joy.

Joy opened it, and inside was a small, stuffed bear with his paw over his mouth. Candace recognized it as one of the stuffed animals Tamara had on display in her room.

"When I was three, my mom gave me that bear, and she told me that when I understood when to listen and when to speak, then I would be wise. As Candace can tell you, it's a lesson I'm still learning. But I thought it was time for WiseBear to help someone else learn."

Joy hugged Tamara. Candace smiled. Things were going really well. She was just starting to hope that she would be able to give her present to Jen despite the fact that she was going last and wouldn't be able to choose the recipient.

Amazingly, when it came to her turn, Jen was the only one left. "This is awesome," Candace said. "I was hoping to give this to you."

Jen opened the Casting Crowns CD. "Some of their music has really inspired me and helped me through some tough times," Candace said.

"Thank you," Jen said, and for a minute Candace thought the other girl was going to cry.

They wrapped up Bible study, and everyone headed home excited about their presents. Jen lingered behind and finally came over to Candace.

"You know how I was having trouble with my friend?" she asked.

"Yes."

"I thought about what you said, and you were right. It's having a close friend that I'm going to miss, not her. I told her that I don't like the lifestyle she's choosing and I didn't want to be a part of it."

"Good for you," Candace said.

"Thanks. It's hard, though. I mean, she's been my only real friend since kindergarten, and I'm not sure how to make a new one."

"Can I give you some advice?" Candace asked.

"Please."

"Think about getting a part-time job. Think The Zone."

Jen's eyes widened. "That place was so cool when we went at Halloween. You really think I could get a summer job there?"

"I'm sure you can. Just make sure you apply by March."

"Thanks!" Jen said.

"She's going to be okay," Tamara said as they watched Jen leave.

"I really do think so," Candace agreed.

❄

The last day of class for the year arrived, and Candace came armed with candy canes. She passed some out in homeroom.

"What, you don't get enough of passing those things out at work?" Tamara asked, pointing to Candace's basket of candy canes.

She shrugged. "They bring people such joy, I figured, why not? Lots of people here could use more happiness in their lives."

"Especially the teachers," Tamara said.

The bell rang and Tamara held out her hands. "Give me some. I want to spread a little cheer from Candy in my next class."

Candace handed her a bunch. "Just remember, one per person."

"Yes, Mom."

Candace found herself passing out candy canes all morning. It made her feel good, and the hours flew by.

When they finally made it to drama, Mr. Bailey was in high spirits. He had brought cake and punch, and it ended up being more of a party than a class. That suited Candace just fine.

When she wasn't worrying about appearing as Aldonza, she was thinking about their plans to bring Christmas to Sue's family.

By the time the bell rang, she bolted and breathed in her first taste of Christmas-break freedom. All five minutes of it before she had to head to her doctor's office and then to work.

❄

She sat in the waiting room impatiently waiting for the doctor to see her. The leg brace was really starting to bother her. It was hot, heavy, and made her itch. She figured she had been a good girl and patient. She deserved to get out of it. Finally, the nurse called her name, and three minutes later the doctor was looking at her knee.

"Christmas break just started," Candace said.

"Hm?"

"I've really been good about the brace. I only take it off to shower. I even wore it all last week and during Winter Formal."

"I'm glad to hear it."

"I'll be glad to hear that I can stop wearing it during the day," she said.

He looked up after a minute. "It looks like everything's healing nicely. I don't think you're going to need any physical therapy."

"I'm glad," Candace said. "What about the brace?"

"As long as you continue to wear it to bed until New Year's, I don't see why you can't go without it during the day."

"Yes!"

"Now, that's not a license to go crazy. Be careful. And if your knee starts to hurt, put the brace back on for a few hours."

"I will," she promised.

"I want you to wear it the rest of the day, and then tomorrow you can try to go without it."

Candace left the doctor's office a few minutes later, and her mom dropped her at work. As she made her way through the park, she smiled at everyone she passed.

"You're in a good mood," Josh noticed when he hunted her up on one of his breaks.

"I get to take this off tomorrow," she said, waving her hand at the brace.

"Wow! We're going to have a lot of celebrating to do tomorrow."

"For what?" Sue asked, appearing as though out of thin air.

"My leg!" Candace said, without missing a beat. "I can take the brace off tomorrow!"

"Congratulations! It's like a Christmas miracle," Sue said with a smile.

"Yes."

"See you ladies later," Josh said, waving as he walked off.

That was a close one, Candace thought as she smiled at Sue.

❄

Later that night she went over the plan on the phone with Josh.

"Roger, Kurt, Pete, and I will bring the tree and the decorations as long as you, Becca, and Martha can handle food and presents," he said.

"We've got it covered," Candace assured him.

"Awesome. This is a good thing you're doing here, Candace."

"*We're* doing," she corrected him.

"Yeah, we just have to make sure they'll all be home tomorrow night."

"I'll ask Sue in the morning," said Candace.

"Good. Let me know once you talk to her."

"Will do."

After they hung up, Candace tried to go to bed, but she found that she was far too excited to sleep. She just prayed that everything would go well and that Sue, Mary, and Gus would be surprised. She wanted so badly to do something nice for them after all that they'd been through.

"Dear God, watch over and protect them all. Help tomorrow night to be a blessing in their lives," she prayed.

She grabbed Mr. Huggles and squeezed him tight. She couldn't wait to see the looks on Gus's and Mary's faces when they opened up their toys. It took an hour but she finally drifted off to sleep.

16

In the morning Candace stared in the mirror at her two legs side by side. They looked a little strange to her without the brace. When she tried to walk, it felt a little awkward because she had gotten used to the extra weight.

She took the stairs slowly, mindful of what the doctor had said about not going crazy. She put her brace and the crutches in the trunk of the car before climbing in. She'd asked her dad to put the presents in the trunk for her. She hadn't driven since the accident, because she couldn't keep her left leg straight and still be close enough to reach the pedals with her right. It felt odd but good to drive again.

When she got to the Santa Zone, she did a slow turn to thunderous applause from the other elves. She decided to still use the stool, though, to avoid putting more stress on her knee.

"Better safe than sorry, I always say," an elf named Calliope told her.

Candace could barely wait until her morning break. When it finally came, she went hunting for Sue. She found her close to the cantina.

"Hey, how's it going?" Candace asked.

"Okay," Sue said. "Look at you! I was just beginning to get used to the brace, and now you look a little off balance."

"I feel a little off balance," Candace admitted.

"How's the candy cane business?"

Candace rolled her eyes. "I'm starting to think I don't ever want to see another candy cane as long as I live."

Sue laughed. "Didn't you say the same thing about candy corn a couple of months ago?"

"I vaguely remember something like that," Candace acknowledged with a laugh.

"And before that wasn't it cotton candy?"

"Probably. So, what are you up to tonight?" she asked, holding her breath as she waited for the answer.

Sue smiled, but her eyes looked tired. "Not much. Just staying home with my brother and sister and trying to get some rest."

"Good, that's good. Resting is good," Candace said, realizing she was babbling.

"Yeah," Sue said. "How about you?"

"I don't know, just hanging out, I guess," Candace said.

"Well, I'll see you later," Sue said.

"Yeah, later," Candace said, trying hard not to smile.

Sue moved away, and Josh approached. "Well?" he asked.

"Home all night," Candace said.

"Awesome. I'll spread the word."

"Thanks, Josh."

Candace could barely contain herself for the next two hours. She couldn't wait to get to Sue's house and see the look on her face when she opened the door.

It seemed like she passed out a million candy canes in those two hours, and yet the kids kept coming. She was so distracted by thoughts of the surprise party, that she handed a candy cane to Becca before she realized what she was doing.

"Thank you!" Becca said.

"Ooh, sorry," Candace said, snatching the sugary treat back.

"Oh, man," Becca said, looking crushed.

"I'm sorry. You know that normally I'd let you keep it, but we've got things to do tonight."

"I know," Becca said. "Josh said we were a go for the party."

"Yup." Candace glanced at her watch. "I'm off now."

"So am I."

"You want to help me do some shopping?" Candace asked.

"Sure."

"Great, let's go."

❄

Candace and Becca headed for the grocery store. Candace pushed the cart, leaning on it a little for support, while Becca plucked things off the shelves.

"I don't think we're going to need four pies," Candace said. "Not unless one of those is just for you."

"Could it be?" Becca asked with a mischievous grin.

"Only if it's sugar free."

"You're no fun."

They grabbed everything else they could think of to make the Christmas feast complete. Martha had already volunteered to cook and bring the turkey.

An hour later Candace parked the car at Sue's house, and she and Becca climbed out. Martha joined them a moment later, and they pulled bags out of the trunk of both cars. A couple feet away the guys were pulling the tree and boxes of decorations out of the bed of Roger's truck.

Candace was excited and nervous at the same time. She prayed that everything would go well.

"You're sure they're home, right?" Kurt asked.

"Yes," Candace said. Suddenly, though, she felt nervous. It would be terrible to have brought everything only to find Sue not home. She had said she wasn't going out, though.

"Lights are on; she should be home," Josh said.

Candace juggled the bags in her arms until she could close her trunk. Then she walked up onto Sue's porch with the others close behind.

Candace stood nervously with the others, clutching her bags of food and presents while Josh reached out and rang the doorbell. She heard voices from inside and moments later Sue opened the door.

"Surprise!" they yelled.

Sue's eyes widened in shock and her fingers gripped the door tight. "Wha—what's going on?" she squeaked.

"Christmas is coming four days early," Candace said.

"I don't know what to say."

"Say come in, it's cold out here," Becca said.

Everyone laughed, and it broke the spell. Sue threw the door open wide, and they all trooped inside. Inside, Sue's younger brother and sister regarded them with wide eyes from the living room couch.

"Which way to the kitchen?" Martha asked.

"This way," Sue said, leading Martha, Becca, and Candace toward it.

Behind her, Candace heard squeals of delight from the children and glanced back to see Roger hauling in the Christmas tree. Josh, Kurt, and Pete followed with boxes of lights and decorations.

"Who wants to help decorate the tree?" Josh asked.

"Me!"

"Me too!"

Candace smiled and walked into the kitchen. By the time they had all set down their bags, the counter was covered.

"What on earth have you all done?" Sue asked.

Candace turned to look at her and saw tears sparkling in her eyes. She reached out and hugged her. "Just brought a little Christmas cheer is all."

"Thank you," Sue whispered, shaking a little as she cried.

"You're welcome," Candace said, starting to tear up herself.

"Sorry to interrupt," Martha said, her voice kindly. "But we brought a few extra presents to unwrap on Christmas day itself," she said, handing Sue a bag.

Sue pulled away and took the bag. "I'll be right back," she said before scurrying off.

"You did a good thing here," Martha said once Sue had left the room.

"I just wish I could have done more," Candace admitted.

It was amazing how many things she took for granted. It made her feel sad and a little guilty. It must have shown on her face, because Becca shook her shoulder.

"No sad faces allowed tonight."

"Sorry."

"Don't make me eat sugar," Becca threatened.

"Make you?" Martha asked, rolling her eyes. "It's almost impossible to stop you."

Becca shrugged and gave them both an impish smile, one with the slightest hint of a sugar craze in it.

Candace reached for the dessert bag. "You didn't ..."

Sure enough, the bag of Christmas-colored Hershey kisses was open. "Oh no," Candace groaned.

Becca's smile got a little wider. "It was just one."

"One is more than enough," Martha said, snatching the bag. "Who let her carry this bag in?"

"What bag?" Sue asked, returning to the kitchen.

"This one," Martha said, waving the bag of chocolate in the air.

Sue went completely white.

"Don't worry. It was just one," Becca said with a little hop.

A commotion from the other room drew their attention, and they all moved to get a view of the living room. The Christmas tree was standing in the middle of the room, and each child had a strand of lights that they were wrapping around the tree, running past each other and squealing.

"Faster, faster!" Kurt urged them on.

"There goes any chance at quiet and dignity," Martha said with a smile.

"I think quiet and dignity are overrated," Candace said, laughing at the sight.

"How're you ladies coming? We're going to be done here before you know it," Josh said.

"I guess we should hurry then," Candace said, turning back to the kitchen.

"What is all this?" Sue asked, waving toward the bags.

"Dinner," Martha said.

"And presents!" Becca chimed in.

Candace grabbed a bag and pulled the presents out of it. She carried them into the living room and started a pile on the floor.

"See that, kids?" Roger asked. "We have to finish decorating so we can put the presents under the tree!"

There was more laughter, and Candace joined in as she raced back into the kitchen for more presents. In a minute she had separated out all the presents and stacked them in the living room. Back in the kitchen the others had emptied the food out of the paper bags.

"We figured we could all have Christmas dinner together a couple days early," Candace explained. "So we brought turkey, stuffing, mashed potatoes, and cranberries."

"Don't forget the pies," Becca said, eyes wide.

"One of which is sugar free," Martha said pointedly.

Becca looked so sad, Candace couldn't help but feel sorry for her.

"You guys didn't have to do this," Sue said.

"Oh hush," Martha said. "You know, any excuse to have a party."

They heated up the food and chilled the sparkling cider. Josh sauntered into the kitchen when they were just finishing.

"That food had better be ready. Tree's gonna be done in five minutes, and if food isn't ready we're setting the kids loose on the presents."

"The food will be ready," Candace said, handing him a stack of plates. "Help me set the table."

Five minutes later they were all sitting down to eat. They all held hands and Josh prayed.

"God, thank you for everything that we have, especially good friends and family. We ask that you bless this dinner and all who are partaking of it. Amen."

"Amen," they all chorused.

Candace picked up the platter in front of her, and soon dishes of food zipped around the table. For five minutes no one said a word as everyone began to scarf down the food.

Pete broke the silence. "You ladies did yourselves proud. I can't remember the last Christmas dinner I had that tasted so good."

"Here, here," Kurt added.

Candace smiled. It had to be one of the strangest holiday meals she had ever had, and she was sharing it with the strangest, coolest people she could hope for. She watched in delight as Mary and Gus stuffed themselves and Sue laughed and laughed. Seeing her look so happy was the best gift Candace could have hoped for.

A half hour later, everyone had pushed their plates away and was groaning and rubbing their bellies. Candace, Becca, Roger, and Martha carried the dishes into the kitchen and began cleaning up while the others played with Mary and Gus in the living room.

"If somebody's got a CD player, I've got Christmas music," she heard Kurt say.

"Who wants to help me set up the train?" Pete asked to squeals of delight.

At last dishes were in the dishwasher, and leftover food was in the fridge.

"I think we should wait awhile before we serve pie," Martha said, and Candace quickly agreed.

"I think it's present time," Josh said, poking his head into the kitchen. "I can't hold these kids back any longer."

"You mean we can't hold you back any longer," Roger joked.

"Hey, I know I saw a present with my name on it," Josh laughed.

"Who's going to pass out the presents?" Becca asked as she hopped into the other room.

"I vote for Pete," Candace said.

"I second that," Martha said.

Candace found herself in the living room sitting between Josh and Kurt on the couch. Everyone else sat on chairs scattered about the room in a loose circle.

Pete handed out a round of presents. Candace looked down at hers. *To Candy, Merry Christmas! Becca.* She gasped when she saw that there was a small heart over the "i" in Christmas. She looked over at Becca. So, she had found the golden candy cane after all! All of her charts and maps and statistical analysis had paid off for her. Candace was glad.

When everyone had a present, Pete shouted, "Let 'er rip!"

There were shouts of laughter, and wrapping paper went flying up into the air. Candace opened her box, and inside was a gold candy cane lapel pin. She laughed and held it up for all to see. "Does this mean I win?" she asked.

Everyone else laughed too.

"Thanks, Becca."

"You're welcome and thank you!" Becca said, waving the box of See's in the air.

Sue gave out a little shriek when she saw it.

"It's okay, they're sugar free," Candace hastened to assure everyone.

Pete passed out the next round of presents, and Candace noticed that Kurt was holding the one from her.

"Let 'er rip!" Pete shouted again.

Kurt opened his present, and a strange look crossed his face. He pulled the watch out slowly and then looked up at Candace. "How did you know?" he asked.

"I had a little help from Santa," she admitted.

"I used to have one just like this. It belonged to my grandfather, but something happened to it."

Candace felt warm inside. Santa had been right.

Candace opened Josh's present and began to laugh hysterically. She held up a tiny trophy and read the inscription out loud, "Candace Thompson. For most visits to The Hospital Zone in a single year!"

Gus and Mary were overwhelmed with excitement by their presents. Mary was clutching a doll. Gus had a basketball in one hand and a large box containing a basketball hoop that could be attached to the house in the other.

"I'll come over and help you put that up tomorrow," Roger told him.

They opened more presents, and Candace loved that Kurt gave her a statue of the Lone Ranger. "It looks like you the day we met!" she said.

The last round of presents finally arrived, and when the paper had fallen to the ground, Candace saw that Roger had actually done it. He had given Becca a huge box of chocolates. Everyone stared for a moment, including Becca.

"They're *not* sugar free," Roger said.

Suddenly, there was a flurry of activity as four people dove at the box of candy and Becca did a backflip over her chair, clutching the candy over her head. She hit the ground running and headed for the front door. "My present! Mine!" she shrieked.

She made it outside, and Pete, Kurt, Josh, and Martha followed. There were grunts, and it sounded like some heavy-duty tackling was going on.

"I did a bad, bad thing," Roger admitted.

Sue sighed. "There goes the neighborhood."

Gus and Mary just stared wide eyed.

Roger stood, a guilty look on his face. "I should go help her."

"Her?" Candace asked.

"Them. Help them get her."

He walked outside, and Candace and Sue burst out laughing.

"One thing's for sure, life is never dull around this crowd," Sue said at last.

"I should think not. Here, let me help you clean up," Candace said as she stood up.

She and Sue grabbed trash bags and started stuffing them full of discarded wrapping paper. They tossed the bows into a small pile under the Christmas tree. When they were nearly done, everyone else trooped back in. There were grass and dirt stains covering most of them. Becca had a wild, defiant look in her eyes, but her hands were empty.

"We've promised to give this to her once she's at home," Josh said, holding the candy box high.

Candace could swear she heard Becca muttering, "My candy," over and over again. Everyone took a trip to the rest-room to wash up as best they could. Then they indulged in pie. Candace couldn't help but feel sorry for Becca as she watched the other girl miserably eat her slice of sugar-free apple pie. When at last dessert was finished and cleaned up, Sue thanked them all again.

"On this happy note, I think I'll say good night," Martha said at last.

"I'll walk out with you," Pete said.

Gus had engaged Roger in an earnest conversation about basketball.

"I need to get going too," Kurt said. He gave Candace a quick kiss before heading out.

"Hey, Roger," Josh said.

"Yeah?"

"Could I trust you to drive Becca home and not give her your gift again until you get there?"

"Yeah, I'm your man," Roger said, jumping to his feet. "I'll be over tomorrow so we can shoot some hoops," he promised Gus.

"Come on, Becca, I'll take you home," he said with the hint of a blush.

"Good night," Becca said, hugging Sue. "Merry Christmas."

"Thank you," Sue said. "Merry Christmas to you too."

Becca and Roger left.

"I hope the two of them go out soon," Josh said with a sigh. "Watching them is driving everyone crazy."

"Tell me about it," Candace said, rolling her eyes. "I thought it was a done deal half a dozen times already."

Sue smiled at them. "It's amazing sometimes how blind or shy people can be. You just never can tell sometimes what will finally wake two people up."

"Will you be able to give me a lift later?" Josh asked Candace. "Roger was kinda my ride."

"No problem."

Gus and Mary finally said good night. Both of them looked exhausted but happy. Sue, Josh, and Candace chatted while they finished cleaning up. At the end, Sue grabbed an empty box and started scooping bows into it from the pile under the tree.

"Hey, what's this?" she asked.

"What?" Josh asked, craning to see what she was holding.

Hanging from one of the bottom branches of the tree was a small, wrapped present.

Sue pulled it off. "It's addressed to me, but it doesn't say who it's from."

"Open it," Candace urged.

Sue sat down and unwrapped the gift. She gasped and then slowly held it up. There in her hand was the golden candy cane.

"Who ... who would give this up?" Sue asked.

Tears flooded Candace's eyes. "I know," she said. After all that hard work, all that searching, and her desperate desire to have the gingerbread house, Becca had given it all away to someone who needed it more.

17

Josh and Candace stayed a little while longer before finally leaving. They ended up heading to a coffee shop to decompress and discuss the evening.

"It was better than I dreamed," Candace said.

"It was awesome. Did you see Gus's face when he opened up the basketball you got him? I was mad that I forgot to bring a camera."

"I should have used my phone to take a picture," Candace said.

"I heard a rumor that you're going to be in *Man of La Mancha*."

"It's true."

"Awesome. You are going to invite everyone to come see it, right?"

"I wasn't planning on it," Candace said with a laugh.

"You should. I think it would be fun. We need to do more stuff outside The Zone like this. You know, something every few months."

"That would be fun," Candace admitted.

"And see, your play is the perfect chance. We can go out to Max's Opera Café afterward."

Candace laughed. "I don't think my performance will quite warrant that."

"Who cares? I want to go to the café," Josh said with a laugh.

Candace smiled and rubbed her knee. It was starting to get a little stiff.

"Do you need me to get you something? Ice? Your brace?"

"No, I probably just need to go home and rest," Candace said.

"You seem to be holding up pretty well," Josh said, standing and dumping his trash into the bin.

"Yeah. It's been awesome."

They got to the car, and Josh gave her directions to his house.

"Kurt said you and Tamara looked gorgeous the other night. I would have loved to have seen you guys all dressed up."

Candace laughed. "I tried to convince Tam to ask you out, but she wouldn't."

"Yeah, she and I would so not work. I like her, I really do, but I think we would drive each other crazy in a bad way."

"Can't blame a girl for trying," Candace said.

When they reached Josh's street, Candace slowed down.

"You can just drop me at the gate," he said.

"What? Don't want me to see where you live?" she joked.

"Nah. Are you kidding? You already know my big secret. What more could I possibly be hiding? It's just late and I don't want to wake mom and dad up."

She pulled over, and he hopped out of the car. "See you later, Candy Cane," he said with a grin before closing the door.

She shook her head. She'd only known Josh a few months, but some days it seemed like a lifetime. She put her foot on the gas and headed for home.

Once home she put the Lone Ranger statue, the trophy from Josh, and the golden candy cane all on her dresser next to her other souvenirs from The Zone. She changed into her pajamas and actually felt a tiny bit better when she strapped on the leg brace.

She was exhausted, but her mind was racing. She replayed the evening, remembering everything that was said and how everyone looked. Operation Christmas Carol had been a success. There was no way she could have pulled it off without her friends.

She felt amazed that she had somehow become part of The Zone community. When she had started working there in the summer, Tamara had been her only real friend. Now there were several people who fit into that category. She thought about what Sue had said about a gift being a wish from the heart.

She closed her eyes and thought of each of her friends. *God, I'd like to give a gift to each of my friends tonight. I'd like to give Roger the courage to tell Becca how he really feels about her. I'd like to give Becca the respect that she deserves. I'd like to give Martha a Christmas surrounded by those who love her. For Pete, I'd like to give the feeling of Christmas all year round. I'd like to give Tamara what she's searching for. For Sue I'd like to give a future that is brighter than her current circumstances. For Josh ... I'm not sure what I would like to give him, but I want you to make his brother's homecoming a blessing to everyone who knows him. And dear God, for Kurt, I'd like to ask for happiness. Amen.*

❄

The next day, spirits were running even higher than usual in the Holiday Zone. Even Santa somehow seemed jollier. Candace was relishing the freedom of her second day without the leg brace. She had even opted to forego the stool. Unlike the day before, she was more confident and beginning to feel like her old self. It was a shame that there were only two more days of this. She was finally feeling like she really had the hang of the whole elf business.

On one of Santa's breaks, Candace got the chance to thank him for the hint about the watch. He smiled at her and winked. "I was glad to help, Candace. I want to thank you for the fine work you've done here. If you ever want to become a full-time elf, look me up."

"Thanks, Santa. Oh, and my best friend wants me to tell you that if you ever need a Mrs. Claus ..."

He laughed, a deep belly laugh that brought a smile to her face. "I have a Mrs. Claus. But you tell Tamara that she'll find her Mr. Right soon enough."

He turned and left, and Candace stared after him. *How did he know her name?* she wondered.

"Earth to Candace?"

She turned around and saw her mother standing there. "Sorry, Mom, I didn't hear you. What's up?"

"I'm heading home. I just had a short shift this morning. Will you need me to pick you up tonight?"

"I'm not sure. I'll see if I can catch a ride with someone."

"Well, give me a call if you can't."

"Thanks, Mom."

With so few days left before Christmas, the elves had gotten official word that they could double the number of presents they were giving out. Candace made full use of the opportunity. Every time she handed a child a present, she couldn't help but see Mary and Gus in her mind. She was so glad that everything had turned out well the night before. She had vowed to help Sue this Christmas season, and she finally had. Still, Becca had been much more generous than she in the long run.

When lunchtime finally came, she headed off toward the Muffin Mansion to talk to Becca. As she walked, Roger caught up with her and fell into step.

"So, how did things go with Becca last night?" she asked.

"Fine. We talked. I dropped her at her house, gave her the candy, and ran."

"Coward."

"That's me."

"Seriously, Roger. When are you going to make a move? Ask her out, kiss her, something?"

"I don't know," he said, voice full of misery. "I have every intention of doing just that, then I get around her and I get all tongue-tied."

As they passed one of the restrooms, Sue came flying out. She threw her arms around both of them in an impromptu hug, and they hugged her back. "Thank you again for everything!" she said. "Mary and Gus couldn't stop talking about it this morning. That was the best Christmas present anyone could ever have given."

"We were glad to help," Roger said, smiling.

"And thank you for offering to come over and help put up the basketball hoop," Sue said.

"No problem, happy to do it. I've got to encourage my fellow athletes in any way possible."

Sue laughed. "It's amazing. You know, sometimes I think this place does something wonderful to people. It makes us all better."

"I couldn't agree more," Candace said with a smile. "I think it's because we get to hang out with such great people."

"I have to get back to it, but I saw you guys and just had to say thank you again. And Roger?"

"Yeah?"

"Ask out Becca. I'm sure she'll say yes."

Roger blushed and nodded.

Candace and Roger continued walking. They reached the Muffin Mansion and found Gib and Becca outside. Becca was standing on a ladder, hanging something over the door.

"What's going on?" Candace asked.

"A little last-minute decoration, as it were," Gib said.

"I'm hanging mistletoe," Becca said brightly. "Is this centered?"

"Yes," Gib said.

Becca finished pushing the tack into place.

"Hey, Roger," Becca said.

"Hey."

Candace rolled her eyes. Gib muttered something under his breath.

"Roger!" Gib growled.

"Yeah?"

"Catch," Gib said before putting his foot on the ladder and shoving.

It wobbled a moment, and Becca shrieked before tumbling backward. She landed in Roger's outstretched arms. He stared at her, and she stared back.

Then, for one agonizing moment, Candace thought he was about to set her on her feet.

"For crying out loud, you idiot, you're standing under the mistletoe!" Gib bellowed.

Roger jerked as if stung. Then he bent down and kissed Becca, and she kissed him back. They stayed like that for a minute.

"That boy's got a wildcat on his hands," Gib muttered to Candace, shaking his head.

"I can't believe you did that. She could have gotten hurt!" Candace said.

Gib shrugged. "What can I say? Kids shouldn't try this at home."

Finally the kiss ended. "Becca, will you—"

"I thought you'd never ask," Becca interrupted him. Then she kissed him.

"Finally," Gib said, shoulders relaxing. "They were driving me crazy with all their mooning around."

Candace grinned, patted Gib on the arm, and headed back to the Holiday Zone, determined to find Josh and tell him the good news. Back in the Holiday Zone, though, the first person she recognized wasn't Josh but Tamara.

"Hey, Tam, what are you doing here?" Candace asked.

"I figure this was a good place to shop for the HTBFs on my list."

"HTBF?" Candace questioned. She thought she was familiar with all Tamara's acronyms, but this was a new one.

"Hard to buy for."

"Ah."

"See, here I can find stuff they won't have seen in the mall or are not likely to have already."

"True."

"I'm sure to find a few things that will work."

"What's the verdict on your evil aunt? Is she coming for Christmas? Do you have to get her something?"

"I should get her something, but I'm not likely to be able to buy her soul back," Tamara said, rolling her eyes. "Yes, she's coming, and so is Trevor. Is it too late to come spend Christmas at your house?"

"It's never too late. I'm just not sure your folks would be happy about it."

"Maybe they'll still be discussing Aunt Liv, and they won't even notice I'm gone."

"Dream on."

"Can't blame me for trying. Well, wish me luck. These presents aren't going to buy themselves."

"Good luck. Don't forget to check out the eco-friendly booth," Candace said.

"I think my Uncle Mike is getting one of their birdfeeders. Speaking of, is your mom here today?"

"No, why?"

"I wanted to do present coordination with her."

"What?"

"Oh come on, Cand. We do it every year."

"Are you serious?"

"Of course. Remember the first Christmas after we became friends?"

"Yeah."

"She and I gave you the same Barbie."

"I didn't mind," Candace said.

"Yeah, yeah. Look. Every year when I think of something cool, she's beaten me to the punch. This year, though, I'm going to win. I've got something so cool there's no way she's thought of it."

"If you're so sure, then why are you worried about coordinating with her?" Candace asked, still amused by the whole idea.

"Because I want her to acknowledge my terminal coolness. Well, that, and it's kinda become a tradition."

Candace laughed. Just when she thought her friends and family couldn't get any weirder, they always found a way to surprise her.

"I'll just have to call her, I guess. Anyway, I can do that later. Now it's time to shop."

"Have fun," Candace said.

"I will. And tell Santa I'll be back to have a few words with him. Save me a candy cane."

"Santa already had a few words for you!" Candace called.

She smiled at Tamara's retreating back. Having two of the same Barbie had never bugged her. She'd just thought of them as twins. It seemed funny to her that it had bugged Tamara enough that she had spent the last thirteen years coordinating gifts with her mom.

She turned and walked over to where Josh stood by the exit to one of the rides. "I dig the costume," she said.

He was dressed in a white snowsuit. "Yeah, I just got off working the Toboggan ride today. I was filling in for someone."

"I heard a bunch of refs went down it backward after park closing two nights ago."

"Guilty as charged," he said, flashing a smile.

"I've got news," Candace said.

"Do tell."

"I just left the Muffin Mansion where Becca and Roger were kissing under the mistletoe."

"Yes! Finally!"

"It's too bad we didn't have a wager on that," she said slyly.

"Aha! I knew it!"

"Knew what?

"I knew this was going to come around to pizza somehow."

"I have no idea what you're talking about. Since you brought it up, though, when are you making me pizza?" she asked.

"Ah! I knew that gift came with a catch," he said.

"Yes, it did. I expect some kind of fabulous gourmet pizza."

"I see. Did you have anything particular in mind?"

"No, I figure you can go through the book and surprise me. Did you really like it, though?"

As she was talking, a guy with a blond crew cut and dressed in jeans and a tight black T-shirt walked up behind Josh. He put a finger over his lips like he didn't want her to say anything. She wasn't sure who he was or what he was planning, but there was something about him that seemed familiar.

"It was awesome!" Josh finished. "I looked it over a little more closely this morning, and I found a couple we have to try."

"I go off overseas to fight for my country so my little brother can flirt with girls," the stranger boomed in a loud voice.

Josh jumped, and a look of wild joy passed over his face. He spun around, shouted something Candace didn't understand, and threw his arms around the other guy.

"Hey, Josh. Good to see you too!"

Candace was stunned. This had to be James, Josh's older brother returned from war. A minute later Josh confirmed that as he turned around, still hugging his brother with his right arm while wiping his eyes with his left.

"Candace, this is James, my big brother. James, this is—"

"Let me guess. Cotton Candy?" he asked with a laugh, extending his hand.

Candace shook it. "Actually, right now Candy Cane is more like it," she said, grinning.

"Josh wrote all about your adventures here at The Zone," James said.

Candace could feel herself blushing as she continued to grin like an idiot. Seeing the two side by side, it was easy to see the resemblance. They had similar facial features and matching sets of broad shoulders. James's hair was a shade darker, and he was maybe an inch taller than Josh. He also gave off a little more of an aggressive, take-charge vibe as compared to Josh's usually laid-back style.

"I didn't think you were supposed to be here until tomorrow," Josh said.

"Got in early. Went home, saw Mom and Dad, changed into my civvies, and came to see you," James said.

Josh hugged him again. "Glad you did."

"So, I heard Mom and Dad are throwing a welcome-home party the day after Christmas."

"Yup." Josh turned to Candace. "You'll come, right?"

"Uh, sure, I guess," Candace said, surprised.

"Of course she'll come. It wouldn't be a proper party without Candy Cane," James said with a wink.

"Why do I have a feeling that wherever the two of you are together, it's a party?" Candace asked.

"He brings out the worst in me," James said.

Josh rolled his eyes. "Oh sure, believe *him*."

Tamara walked up holding a sequined Santa hat in her hand. "Hey, Candace, I'll make a great Mrs. Claus. Check it out," she said.

"Cool. Hey, Tamara, I'd like you to meet someone. This is James, Josh's brother."

Tamara turned to look at James, and her entire body seemed to jerk. Her eyes widened and her lips parted. She pressed the Santa hat over her heart and just stared.

Candace was getting embarrassed until she realized James was just staring too.

"James, this is Candace's friend, Tamara," Josh said.

Still, the two of them just stared at each other. Josh and Candace exchanged a quick look. Josh cleared his throat, and James offered his hand. "Pleased to meet you, Tamara."

She shook it. "Likewise, James," she said.

The moment seemed to stretch on forever.

Josh clamped a hand on James's shoulder. "Okay, well, we've got to get out of here. Need to spend some time with the parents and keep them from planning an unbelievably epic-sized party. We'll catch you ladies later."

"You'll come to my welcome-home party?" he asked Tamara.

"Wouldn't miss it," she said.

James smiled briefly at Candace before turning and accompanying his brother out of the Holiday Zone. She watched them go, and a little chill danced up her spine. Something had just happened, and it both excited and frightened her.

Suddenly, Tamara gasped as though she had been holding her breath. "Now that is so right," she whispered.

18

After work Candace got a ride home with Tamara. All the way there, Tamara was quiet. When they pulled up outside Candace's house, she suddenly asked, "How are we supposed to dress for the party?"

"I have no idea," Candace said.

"Call Josh and ask him."

"Okay."

There was a pause while Tamara looked at her expectantly. "You mean, right now?"

"Yes!"

Candace got out her cell phone and called Josh. "Hey, quick question. What's the dress code for the party?"

"Good question. Can I find out and get back to you?"

Candace glanced over at Tamara. "Um, I kinda need to know now."

"Is Tamara still freaking out?"

"You could say that."

"So's James. Here, hold on a second."

Candace waited, and less than a minute later Josh was back. "I was told semiformal."

"Semiformal? Great."

"I'll email you the time and the restaurant and stuff."

"I'd appreciate it. I gotta go deal with some things."

"Yeah, me too."

"Later."

"Bye."

She hung up. "Semiformal."

Tamara nodded. "Okay."

Candace went to open her door, but Tamara grabbed her arm. "What am I going to wear?" she asked.

"A dress?" Candace guessed, smiling.

"This is not funny!" Tamara said, eyes wide. "This is serious. What am I going to wear?"

"You could wear the red dress that you wore to Winter Formal."

"No, I can't! This has to be something special, something perfect. We have to go shopping. Right now."

"Um, Tam? I'm kinda in an elf costume here," Candace pointed out.

"So?"

"Tam! I'm not going to the mall like this! I'll have kids mobbing me, and no candy canes to appease them with."

"Okay, go change. I'll wait."

Candace was sure Tamara had flipped out, but she decided the best course of action would be to humor her. She ran inside, threw on some different clothes, and was back within five minutes.

Once they reached the mall, it took twenty minutes just to find a parking space. This was the kind of chaos Candace had tried so hard to avoid by shopping early. Once inside they headed straight for the dress shop where they had shopped a couple of weeks earlier. It was relatively uncrowded.

"I need that white dress," Tamara said. "Help me find it."

Twenty minutes later they still hadn't found it. "I need it!" Tamara wailed.

"They have other dresses, some of them white even. Why don't you try one of them on?" Candace urged, her friend's despair hurting her.

"Not the same! I knew that dress was right for something, not Winter Formal, but something! I should have bought it then!"

"Can I help you, ladies?" a saleswoman asked.

"I'm looking for a white dress that was here a couple of weeks ago. Floor length, halter neck, slit up the side, white beading."

"I think we sold that dress."

"This is what I get for trying to buy dresses off the rack!" Tamara wailed.

Candace was stunned. She had never seen her like this before. Worse, she didn't know how to help her.

Another salesgirl walked out of the dressing room area carrying several dresses. One of them looked familiar. "Tam, is that it?" Candace asked, pointing.

Tamara looked and then ran over and practically pounced on the startled girl. "Give me that white dress!"

Speechless, she surrendered it, and Tamara ran to the register. The first saleswoman moved to ring it up. "Wait! I almost forgot."

Tamara ran back to one of the racks, yanked free the burgundy dress that had looked good on Candace, and returned to the counter.

"Now go," she said.

Everyone in the store was visibly rattled. Even Candace wanted to take a step or two backward.

"Wait!" she screeched again.

Everyone in the store—customers and workers alike—froze. "Candace, do you have shoes that will go with this?"

"Yes," Candace croaked. She had no idea if she did or not, but she was too afraid to say no.

"And jewelry?"

"Yes," she said with more confidence.

"Okay. Go."

In all her life, Candace never saw a salesperson move so quickly. Less than sixty seconds later they were on their way back to the car. Once in the car, Tamara slumped back in the seat.

"That was a close one," she said.

"It sure was," Candace agreed, still eyeing her suspiciously.

"You have to come to my house and help me pick out jewelry, shoes, everything."

"Okay."

Several minutes later she was standing in the middle of Tamara's closet holding a pair of white high-heeled shoes with open toes. "Definitely these."

Tamara tried on the shoes with the dress and seemed satisfied. "Hair up or down?" was her next question.

"Up. Has to be."

"And jewelry?"

"That silver snowflake necklace you got last Christmas."

"You are a genius!" Tamara said, hugging her hard.

When Tamara let go, Candace sat down on the bed. She asked hesitantly, "Do you want to talk about James?"

"Even his name is perfect," Tamara said.

Candace sensed that it was not the time to have any sort of rational conversation. Instead, she helped pick out the rest of the jewelry, realizing the best she could hope for was a quick escape.

When she finally did make it home, she had an email from Josh. The party for his brother was going to start at seven p.m. at the Stinking Rose, an upscale restaurant named for its primary recipe ingredient: garlic. Josh's family had reserved the entire place for the event.

Candace smirked to herself. Tamara was going to love this. She would be beautiful, dressed to the nines ... and reeking of garlic. She decided to wait to tell her about the location. Tamara had been so out of her mind when she had dropped

Candace off, Candace doubted Tamara would understand if she told her now.

She fired off an IM to Josh when she noticed he was online.

Luv Stinking Rose. Been 2x.

Ditto. Luv part.

T bought us new dresses for it.

Right on! Got a new vest 4 tux.

So much 4 semiformal.

Trust me. This is semi. Fully would include top hat and gloves.

LOL

Not joking

ROFLOL

Just you wait till J & T get married.

U really think so?

Don't know. J never acted like that with a girl before.

Same for T with a guy.

Pretty funny

Speak 4 yourself. U didn't have 2 deal w/ her.

Yeah. But I had 2 deal with him.

Bummer.

Gotta run. Lots to do B4 tomorrow.

TTFN.

Hasta.

❄

It was the day before Christmas Eve. The park was only open until four p.m. when it shut down to get ready for the referee Christmas Party. Candace went home to change clothes and pick up her parents. The Christmas Party was an event where families were welcomed.

When they arrived back at the park, someone handed each of them a goody bag filled with Zone Christmas gifts and memorabilia. They made their way to the auditorium in the Holiday Zone where the evening's festivities would begin.

Candace and her parents found seats close to the stage and settled in. In the row in front of them were Roger and Gib. Candace said hello to them and introduced both her parents. Fifteen minutes later Freddie McFly put on a special show full of inside jokes about life at The Zone, which had everyone laughing so hard they were practically crying.

When the show was over, John Hanson took to the stage. The gingerbread house was wheeled onto the stage next to him, and everyone roared in approval.

"It's my privilege tonight to welcome you to the annual Christmas party," he said. "There are a lot of activities and special treats planned tonight. First, however, there are some people who need to be recognized. We have narrowed down the field in the scholarship competition."

Candace leaned forward slightly. She had only recently discovered that Josh had entered her in that competition. She had doodled a ride concept she called Balloon Races, and he had entered it. The winner got to have their ride built and a full scholarship to Florida Coast University.

"The five finalists for the Game Master scholarship competition have been selected. They are Martin Lamb, Barbara Reynolds, Rick Paulson, Scott Charleston, and Candace Thompson!"

A deafening roar went up from the crowd, and both her parents hugged her at the same time.

A finalist! She could scarcely believe it. Yet it had to be true. She had heard her name, and referees around her were smiling and waving at her. Both Gib and Roger grabbed her hands and shook them enthusiastically.

"Congratulations to all of you. We'll conduct interviews in a few weeks."

Interviews? Candace wasn't sure she liked the sound of that.

"And now, the moment you've been waiting for, the winner of the Golden Candy Cane!"

Sue walked out onto the stage holding the golden candy cane aloft, and Candace began clapping with everyone else. John handed Sue a large envelope that looked completely stuffed.

"As the winner of the golden candy cane, you get gift certificates for several grocery stores, restaurants, movie chains, and theme parks. And you also get a five-thousand-dollar Visa gift card. Of course," he said with a smile, "and finally, you get the life-size gingerbread house!"

Everyone in the auditorium jumped to their feet and shouted in approval. Tears streamed freely down Candace's cheeks, and she didn't care.

John handed the microphone over to Sue.

"I don't know how to say thank you for all of this. It's overwhelming. The Zone has already given me so much: a good job, dear friends, and now this. It's too much. And I owe it all to Becca. This is really her golden candy cane and not mine," Sue said. "So, Becca, as far as I'm concerned this gingerbread house is all yours."

There was an inhuman shriek that Candace figured had to be coming from Becca. The next thing she knew she saw Becca bounce onto the stage and then launch herself at the gingerbread house. She landed on the roof where she begin gnawing on one of the shingles.

Gib sighed. "We're going to need a bigger net."

Candace just stared in fascinated horror. The roof of the house was not designed to support the weight of a person. With a groan it gave way, and Becca fell through into the house. A moment later they heard insane giggling coming from inside.

"On the other hand, maybe it would be best to leave her in there for a while," Gib noted grimly.

"That's my girlfriend!" Roger said proudly.

Around them, people laughed and then applauded.

On stage, John Hanson doubled over with laughter. Finally he took the microphone that Sue handed back to him. "I think the only thing I can add to that is 'Merry Christmas.'"

And from inside the gingerbread house Becca shouted, "God bless us, every one."

19

They stayed at the park until almost midnight, eating junk food and riding the rides. Candace managed to introduce her parents to everyone she knew at The Zone. By far the coolest thing, though, was that they all got to ride the Glider coaster backward.

She had agreed to help out by working her old cotton candy cart for an hour. Only she was distributing candy canes and hot chocolate. Most people took a turn doing something for an hour, so that the rides could be open. Her parents went on some rides and then came back to get her when her hour was over. Fortunately it was the best hour she had ever spent running the cart.

Candace was sad when they finally headed home, but she crawled into bed and fell asleep quickly.

❄

The next day was by far the best. It was Christmas Eve. Candace had enough presents left over to hand out one to every kid who stopped by her. Not a single one of them was rude, either. Her shift seemed to fly by. It was with a touch of sadness that she handed the candy cane basket over to Lisa for the last time. She turned to go.

"Candace?"

"Yes?" she asked.

Lisa had a strange look on her face, like she couldn't decide what she wanted to say. They locked eyes for a long minute before Lisa looked away. "Merry Christmas."

"Merry Christmas to you too, Lisa," Candace said.

She went to the Locker Room where she grabbed her clothes and other things. She changed in the restroom and then headed for the costume department.

She walked into the costume building where she handed her elf costume to Janet.

"Don't look so sad," Janet said, "you'll be back."

Candace smiled at her. "I really liked being an elf."

"It suited you," Janet said, smiling back.

Candace left and walked back to the Holiday Zone. She walked up to her mother's booth and found that she was already closing up shop.

Candace couldn't help but feel sad as she helped her mom pack up the stuff from her booth. It had been cool to see her occasionally. It had also been cool to be a part of Christmas at The Zone. She found she was going to miss it, even if she didn't want to see a candy cane for a long, long time.

"You know, I'm actually going to miss this place," her mom said.

"It grows on you," Candace said with a smile.

"Yeah. We should come back in a couple of days and ride some rides."

"Careful, Mom, you're starting to talk like a Zoner."

"I guess I am at that," she laughed. "And why not? This is a great place. I didn't realize how great until this past month."

In a strange way, neither had Candace. Stranger still, it was the first time she was leaving the park without a strong feeling that she'd be back. She had figured she'd get another summer job at the park, but summer seemed a long ways away.

Sue came by with the dolly to help them move everything back to the van.

"Didn't we just do this?" Candace joked.

Sue smiled. "Feels like it. And yet, I still can't believe tomorrow's Christmas."

"Neither can I."

"Would you and Gus and Mary want to come to our house for Christmas tomorrow?" Candace's mom asked.

"No, but thank you. The prize package I got last night included some gasoline cards. We're going to leave after I get off work tonight and drive to Arizona to spend it with a great-aunt we have there."

"That sounds like fun. Drive safe."

"We will."

Soon the van was packed up, and Candace and her mom headed home.

"We're barely going to have enough time to change before your father's family gets here," her mom noted.

"Maybe we can put them to work unloading the van."

"Good one! I like it."

When they got home they each unloaded half a dozen boxes from the van before heading upstairs to change. Candace had just finished when the doorbell rang. She hurried downstairs to find Tamara in front of the Christmas tree, present in hand.

"Hey, Tam!"

"We hadn't said when we were exchanging, so I thought we could do it now. I can't stay long; family's coming over tonight for me too."

Candace dove under the tree and came back up with Tamara's present.

They both sat down on the couch and swapped. Candace loved shopping for Tamara. There was nothing her friend needed, and nothing she wanted that she wouldn't get. That left Candace free to buy her crazy, strange, wonderful things as whim moved her.

"You first," Candace urged.

Tamara opened her present and started shrieking in delight as she pulled a tiara out of the box. It was silver and covered with tiny snowflakes.

Candace hugged her. "You'll always be the Christmas queen to me."

Tamara wiped away tears. "This will go great with the white dress."

"I know, and I bought this weeks ago!"

"Well done. Your turn."

Candace unwrapped a medium-size box and lifted the lid. "Oh my gosh!"

"I know how much you love *A Christmas Carol*, so I bought you every version that's on DVD, including that one with Bill Murray, *Scrooged*."

Candace had to laugh. "This is so cool. I haven't even seen half of these!"

"I hadn't heard of half of them."

"Will you watch them with me?"

"Sure, why not? Just not tonight."

"Deal."

"There is something else that goes with them, though."

Candace looked at Tamara, a strange tingling sensation starting on the back of her neck. Usually she could count on Tamara not to overwhelm her completely with gifts on her birthday or Christmas. Every once in a while, though, Tamara did something completely over the top. Candace had a feeling something big was coming.

"I think what you did for Sue was really cool. You know, it was awesome, thoughtful, generous. It got me thinking about what you would really like for Christmas."

"Which is what?" Candace asked.

"Well, I had a long talk with my parents. Sue doesn't know it yet, but she's about to be offered a full ride at Cal State."

Candace sat blinking for a moment and then threw her arms around Tamara. "That's the best Christmas present ever!"

"I thought you'd like it," Tamara said, hugging her back.

Just then, the first group of relatives arrived.

"That's my cue to exit," Tamara said.

"Thanks."

"No problem. Call me tomorrow."

Candace couldn't stop grinning like an idiot the rest of the night.

❄

Candace woke to the sound of coffee brewing downstairs, and in five minutes was perched on the couch staring at the presents under the tree. Yawning, her dad entered the room with a cup of coffee in hand. Her mom was right behind him, rubbing her eyes.

"At least it's not five thirty. That was awful when you'd wake us up that early," her dad said.

"Don't forget the year of four thirty," her mom chimed in.

"Hey, I remember that year. You made me go back to bed," Candace protested.

"We were so wise then," her dad said.

As they opened their presents, she couldn't help but think of Sue and Gus and Mary. She hoped they'd made it to Arizona all right and that they were having a wonderful Christmas.

Josh called to wish her Merry Christmas, and she called Tamara and chatted for a few minutes before leaving a message for Kurt on his cell. As friends and family dropped by in the afternoon, the happy glow of Christmas continued to fill Candace's heart. She couldn't help but start to get a little anxious, though, about what James's welcome-home party the next night was going to entail.

❄

When it came time to get dressed for the party, Candace went to Tamara's house. She had to admit the burgundy dress was really growing on her, and Tamara looked stunning in white. They both did their hair up, and Tamara wore the tiara Candace had given her for Christmas.

"We do look great," Candace admitted at last.

"At least at the Stinking Rose it won't matter what I eat because we'll all reek of garlic," Tamara said cheerily. She was much calmer than Candace had anticipated, in light of the shopping hysterics a few days earlier.

They drove to the restaurant and got a good parking space.

Candace was nervous as she and Tamara walked inside. There were nearly a hundred people seated at tables around the room. She could see Josh with his family at a table at the far end. He looked great in his tuxedo. He gave her a little wave, and she waved back.

"So, tell me more about Josh's brother," Tamara asked as they sat down.

"Well, I know he's almost twenty-three."

"And I'll be eighteen next week. So, he's within the five-year rule?"

"Yes." Tamara had a rule. She wouldn't date any guy who was more than five years older (or younger) than her. This was the first time a guy had ever pushed the limit.

"He got his bachelor's degree in like two and a half years."

"Smart, industrious, a guy who knows what he wants and goes after it," Tamara commented.

"Yeah, I guess so."

"What else?"

"He then signed up to serve in the army. He went to Iraq, and he was just discharged last week."

"A patriot who understands duty, honor, country," Tamara said, a dreamy look on her face.

"Seriously, Tam, don't you think he's a little too old?"

Tamara glared at her. "Less than five years. That might seem like a big difference now, but it won't be in a couple more years. Besides, everyone knows women mature faster than men. And I could definitely use a mature guy who knows what he wants out of life and makes things happen."

Candace smiled. There was no stopping Tamara when she was like this. She also could teach people a thing or two about going after what you wanted.

"What about Santa, though?" Candace teased. "I thought you were planning on being Mrs. Claus."

Tamara was staring at something over Candace's shoulder. Her jaw was hanging and her eyes were bulging. Suddenly she smacked Candace in the arm.

"Ow! What was that for?"

"Do you see what I see?"

Candace turned and saw what had made Tamara stare. There was James, the man of the hour, the returning hero, and he was dressed in a Santa Claus suit five times too big for him and passing out presents to guests.

"No way," Candace breathed.

There he was, larger than life. Even if Candace hadn't believed in signs, the sight of him as Santa Claus would have made her sit up and take note.

James looked up and saw them both staring at him. He walked straight over. Candace could hear Tamara making strangling sounds in her throat.

He smiled briefly at Candace before taking Tamara's hand. "You look like the very spirit of Christmas," he said. "You have brightened this evening by your presence. Thank you for being here. I have to go greet people, but please, I want to speak with you later tonight."

Tamara nodded.

He smiled, kissed the back of her hand, and walked away.

"What just happened?" Tamara asked breathlessly.

"I think an authority figure just proclaimed you Christmas queen," Candace said with a grin.

"Mrs. James . . . what is Josh's last name?" Tamara asked suddenly.

Candace sucked in her breath. "I think Josh's dad is about to make a toast."

Tamara turned to look and then gasped. "No way!"

"I'd like to thank everyone for coming out tonight to help us celebrate James's safe return. We're just so happy he's home and very, very proud of him. So, James, here's to you." He lifted his glass.

Around the room, people also lifted their glasses and many said, "Here, here!"

Candace drank and then put her glass down on the table, afraid to look Tamara in the eye.

"You didn't tell me Josh's parents were famous!" Tamara said.

"It wasn't my secret to tell," Candace said quietly.

Waiters appeared with trays of food, which they set down at each table. Dinner consisted of soup, salad, appetizer, entrée, and dessert, all garlic-laced—except for the dessert. The food was delicious, and, for the most part, the garlic flavor blended subtly into the background.

Tamara was uncharacteristically quiet while she ate. Candace noticed though that after every other bite Tamara turned to try and get a glimpse of James.

As soon as dinner was over, James came back over and sat down next to Tamara. Moments later the two were deep in discussion. Candace got up and walked outside to get some fresh air.

Josh must have had the same thought because that was where she found him. She had to admit that he looked really good in a tuxedo. It was a change from the type of clothes that she normally saw him in. Although she saw him as a more relaxed kind of guy, the tux really did suit him and he wore it like he was used to it.

"James and Tamara were busy talking, so I figured it would be a good time to make myself scarce," Candace said.

"I take it Tamara now knows my secret," Josh said.

"Yeah. She won't tell anyone, though."

"That's cool."

"It's a great party," Candace said.

"Yeah."

"Speaking of, my parents have decided to have a game night New Year's Eve to break in their new board game."

"That sounds like fun."

"I hope so, because they're really insistent that I invite you."

Josh smiled. "Whose team do I have to play on?"

"Dad tried to call dibs, but I told him he was out of luck. You and I are a package deal as far as game night is concerned."

"I like that. Sounds cool. I'd love to come."

"You sure it will be okay with your family?"

"Yeah. James has declared that what he wants to do is catch up on a bunch of the movies he hasn't seen."

"That sounds like fun. I know you like movies, and I know how much you've missed him."

"Yeah, but now that he's home, he and I can go to the movies anytime. How many opportunities will I get to help your family break in a new game? Sorry, gotta say it. The choice seems like a no-brainer."

"I thought that was my line," Candace said.

"I'm not above stealing good lines."

They were quiet for a minute as they took in the beauty of the night. It was always so easy to be with Josh. They could talk for hours or just be quiet, and it was okay either way. She thought about Tamara and James back in the restaurant and wondered how things were going. She had never seen Tamara so smitten before.

"I'm sad that Christmas is over," Candace finally admitted. There was so much more that she wanted to say, but somehow that was all she could find the words for.

"You know, Easter's not that far away," Josh said.

"In your world, all the holidays live next door to each other, don't they?" Candace asked.

"Wouldn't have it any other way. So, seriously. You gonna work at The Zone over spring break?"

"I'll still be recovering from Christmas break," Candace said. She had meant it as a joke, but it didn't seem funny once she said it.

"Come on, it'll be fun. The chocolate eggs, the Easter pageant ... can't miss it."

"Not even you can talk me into it this time, Josh."

"But I'll bet someone can."

"I doubt it. Besides, I think I've now passed out every food item with candy in the title. That's it, I'm done."

"Come on. I can think of other candy things. What about candy buttons?"

"Nope, I checked. We don't sell candy buttons at The Zone," she said, a little thrill of victory running through her.

"Candy cigarettes?"

"What? They don't even make those anymore," Candace said, jolted out of her melancholy. "And even if they do, The Zone wouldn't sell them."

Josh leaned close. "Okay, you win that one. But I know for a fact we sell candy apples."

Candace groaned. "I completely forgot about the apples!"

Josh smiled and leaned back. "That's okay, they didn't forget about you."

"Great, it's going to be me, spring break, and the candy apples. What more could a girl want?"

He gave her a strange look and said softly, "That remains to be seen."

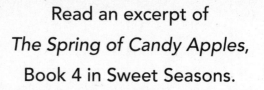

Read an excerpt of
The Spring of Candy Apples,
Book 4 in Sweet Seasons.

Candace couldn't believe how nervous she felt as she headed for The Zone and her first shift at the Candy Counter. In some ways it was just as bad as getting her first job there. Unlike the other jobs she'd had at The Zone, this one didn't come with a built-in expiration date. She was there until she quit. *Or at least until they fire me*, she thought ruefully.

She arrived at the park and made her way toward the store. She had just reached it when she spotted Josh, jogging toward her with a camera in hand.

"What are you doing?" she asked.

He grinned. "Just wanted to get a picture of Candy's first day at the Candy Counter."

She didn't want to, but she couldn't help smiling back at him. "Fine, but just one picture."

"Okay, now stand under the sign," he instructed.

She positioned herself under the *Candy* in the sign and struck a pose.

"Beautiful," he said as he took the picture.

He moved to show it to her on the screen. She laughed when she saw herself.

"Oh yeah, this is going to make a great addition to The Zone Yearbook," he said.

"What?" she asked, the laughter dying on her lips.

"The yearbook. Comes out at the end of May each year."

"You're kidding," she said.

"Nope."

"I've never heard of a Zone yearbook!"

"Candy, there are lots of things here you've never heard of. Still, you're going to be pretty popular in the book this year."

"Give me the camera."

"So you can delete the picture? I don't think so. Besides, isn't it time for your shift?" he asked.

"Fiend."

"That's friend," he corrected.

She rolled her eyes and stepped into the store.

"Surprise!"

Candace jumped backward as dozens of people shouted in unison. Behind her, Josh put a hand on her shoulder and shoved her forward.

Bewildered, she took in the scene. Balloons floated from every hand, and huge banner said Happy Birthday & Welcome Aboard! Everywhere she looked she saw familiar faces of friends and coworkers.

"What's going on?" she asked.

"Well, someone let slip that your birthday is coming up," said Martha. "And then you became a regular non-seasonal employee, and it just seemed like a good excuse to celebrate."

"You guys! Wow, thank you!" she said, humbled and overwhelmed.

"So, I take it you didn't see the sign on the door that said Closed for Private Party?" Becca asked.

"Nope, she was too busy trying to get me to delete her picture," Josh said proudly.

She turned on him and pounded him in the chest with a fist. "You big faker. I knew there wasn't a yearbook!"

"Oh no, there's a yearbook," Pete, the crazy train engineer, spoke up. "I'm guessing you're going to be all over it this year."

"Great," Candace said with a shake of her head. "Okay, so who actually works here?" she asked.

Several hands shot up around the room, and soon Candace's newest coworkers were making their way forward to introduce themselves. Names and faces blurred by for a minute, and Candace realized that she was never going to remember them. Oh well, there'd be plenty of time to get to know everyone later, she decided.

Once the introductions were finished, Becca wheeled out a cake. On top of it her nickname, Candy, was spelled out in a variety of different candies. She smiled, blew out the candles, and received the first piece. It was strawberry cake and amazingly good.

Candace gradually made her way around the store, trying to thank everyone. She finally bumped into Roger.

"Happy almost birthday," he said.

"Thanks. How are you doing?"

"Pretty good. It looks like I'm going to get a sports scholarship to college."

"Roger, that's amazing!" It really was. When she first had met Roger he had been the klutziest guy in the park. Their team had won the summer Scavenger Hunt though, and it had given Roger the confidence he needed.

"So, Roger, I hear there's a talent show coming up. How about getting the team back together?" she asked.

He squirmed slightly. "I'm sorry, Candace. That would be fun, but I'm trying to get a job at the Muffin Mansion. If I get it, I'll be on their team."

"Becca told me they almost never have openings."

"One of the ladies, Sally Lunn, is retiring."

"Wow, really?"

"Yeah. She's seventy. So that means there's going to be an opening, and I want to be the one to get it."

"So you can spend more time with Becca?"

He nodded.

"Good for you! I hope they pick you."

"Me too," he said.

Muffin Mansion referees did all the park activities together. It was a very close-knit group. They were fiercely competitive and completely loyal to each other.

"Hey, stranger," Sue said.

"Hey!" Candace said, giving Sue a quick hug.

"I've been meaning to hunt you down. I'm having a slumber party for my birthday next Friday night. Do you think there's any way you could come?"

It was a long shot, given Sue's brother and sister, but it never hurt to ask.

"I'll see what I can do. A couple of parents owe me some sleepover favors."

"That would so rock!"

"So has anyone told you about the talent show yet?" Sue asked.

"Just found out about it," Candace admitted. "Have you got a team yet?"

"Yeah, Pete, Traci, Corinne from food services, and I signed up last week."

"Oh," Candace said, unable to hide her dismay.

Sue smiled. "We put down your name too, just in case."

"You guys are the best," Candace said, hugging her again.

"Pete had a sneaking suspicion you'd be back. I knew you'd be the last one to hear about the talent show."

"Well, you were both right," Candace said. "What's our talent?"

A Sweet Seasons Novel from Debbie Viguié!

They're fun! They're quirky! They're Sweet Seasons—unlike any other books you've ever read. You could call them alternative, God-honoring chick lit. Join Candy Thompson on a sweet, light-hearted, and honest romp through the friendships, romances, family, school, faith, and values that make a girl's life as full as it can be.

The Summer of Cotton Candy
Book One

Softcover • ISBN: 978-0-310-71558-0

The Fall of Candy Corn
Book Two

Softcover • ISBN: 978-0-310-71559-7

The Spring of Candy Apples
Book Four

Softcover • ISBN: 978-0-310-71753-9

Book 4 coming soon!

Pick up a copy today at your favorite bookstore!

Visit www.zondervan.com/teen

Forbidden Doors

A Four-Volume Series from Bestselling Author Bill Myers!

Some doors are better left unopened.

Join teenager Rebecca "Becka" Williams, her brother Scott, and her friend Ryan Riordan as they head for mind-bending clashes between the forces of darkness and the kingdom of God.

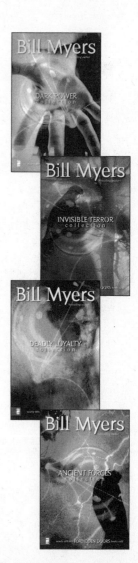

Dark Power Collection
Volume One

Softcover • ISBN: 978-0-310-71534-4

Contains books 1–3: *The Society, The Deceived,* and *The Spell*

Invisible Terror Collection
Volume Two

Softcover • ISBN: 978-0-310-71535-1

Contains books 4–6: *The Haunting, The Guardian,* and *The Encounter*

Deadly Loyalty Collection
Volume Three

Softcover • ISBN: 978-0-310-71536-8

Contains books 7–9: *The Curse, The Undead,* and *The Scream*

Ancient Forces Collection
Volume Four

Softcover • ISBN: 978-0-310-71537-5

Contains books 10–12: *The Ancients, The Wiccan,* and *The Cards*

Echoes from the Edge

A New Trilogy from Bestselling Author Bryan Davis!

This fast-paced adventure fantasy trilogy starts with murder and leads teenagers Nathan and Kelly out of their once-familiar world as they struggle to find answers to the tragedy. A mysterious mirror with phantom images, a camera that takes pictures of things they can't see, and a violin that unlocks unrecognizable voices ... each enigma takes the teens farther into an alternate universe where nothing is as it seems.

Beyond the Reflection's Edge
Book One

Softcover • ISBN: 978-0-310-71554-2

After sixteen-year-old Nathan Shepherd's parents are murdered during a corporate investigation, he teams up with a friend to solve the case. They discover mirrors that reflect events from the past and future, a camera that photographs people who aren't there, and a violin that echoes unseen voices.

Eternity's Edge
Book Two

Softcover • ISBN: 978-0-310-71555-9

Nathan Shepherd's parents are alive after all! With the imminent collapse of the universe at hand, due to a state called interfinity, Nathan sets out to find them. With Kelly at his side, he must balance his efforts between searching for his parents and saving the world. Will Nathan be reunited with his parents?

Book 3 coming soon!

Pick up a copy today at your favorite bookstore!

Visit www.zondervan.com/teen

The Shadowside Trilogy by Robert Elmer!

Those who live in lush comfort on the bright side of the small planet Corista have plundered the water resources of Shadowside for centuries, ignoring the existence of Shadowside's inhabitants, who are nothing more than animals. Or so the Brightsiders have been taught. It will take a special young woman to expose the truth—and to help avert the war that is sure to follow—in the exciting Shadowside Trilogy, the latest sci-fi adventure from Robert Elmer.

Trion Rising

Book One

Softcover • ISBN: 978-0-310-71421-7

When the mysterious Jesmet, whom the authorities brand as a Magician of the Old Order, begins to connect with Oriannon, he is banished forever to the shadow side of their planet Corista.

The Owling

Book Two

Softcover • ISBN: 978-0-310-71422-4

Life is turned upside down on Corista for 15-year-old Oriannon and her friends. The planet's axis has shifted, bringing chaos to Brightside and Shadowside. And Jesmet, the music mentor who was executed for saving their lives, is alive and promises them a special power called the Numa—if they'll just wait.

Book 3 coming soon!

Pick up a copy today at your favorite bookstore!

Visit www.zondervan.com/teen

Share Your Thoughts

With the Author: Your comments will be forwarded to the author when you send them to *zauthor@zondervan.com*.

With Zondervan: Submit your review of this book by writing to *zreview@zondervan.com*.

Free Online Resources at
www.zondervan.com/hello

 Zondervan AuthorTracker: Be notified whenever your favorite authors publish new books, go on tour, or post an update about what's happening in their lives.

 Daily Bible Verses and Devotions: Enrich your life with daily Bible verses or devotions that help you start every morning focused on God.

 Free Email Publications: Sign up for newsletters on fiction, Christian living, church ministry, parenting, and more.

 Zondervan Bible Search: Find and compare Bible passages in a variety of translations at www.zondervanbiblesearch.com.

 Other Benefits: Register yourself to receive online benefits like coupons and special offers, or to participate in research.